ChangelingPress.com

Stunner/ Havoc Duet
A Bones MC Romance
Marteeka Karland

Stunner/ Havoc Duet
A Bones MC Romance
Marteeka Karland

All rights reserved.
Copyright ©2021 Marteeka Karland

ISBN: 9798492818197

Publisher:
Changeling Press LLC
315 N. Centre St.
Martinsburg, WV 25404
ChangelingPress.com

Printed in the U.S.A.

Editor: Katriena Knights
Cover Artist: Marteeka Karland

The individual stories in this anthology have been previously released in E-Book format.

No part of this publication may be reproduced or shared by any electronic or mechanical means, including but not limited to reprinting, photocopying, or digital reproduction, without prior written permission from Changeling Press LLC.

This book contains sexually explicit scenes and adult language which some may find offensive and which is not appropriate for a young audience. Changeling Press books are for sale to adults, only, as defined by the laws of the country in which you made your purchase.

Table of Contents

Stunner (Bones MC 9) 4
   Chapter One 5
   Chapter Two 20
   Chapter Three 30
   Chapter Four 41
   Chapter Five 57
   Chapter Six 70
   Chapter Seven 82
   Chapter Eight 95
   Chapter Nine 108
Havoc (Salvation's Bane MC 4) 117
   Chapter One 118
   Chapter Two 131
   Chapter Three 146
   Chapter Four 162
   Chapter Five 171
   Chapter Six 183
   Chapter Seven 196
   Chapter Eight 207
   Chapter Nine 217
Marteeka Karland 230
Changeling Press E-Books 231

Stunner (Bones MC 9)
Marteeka Karland

Suzie -- I'm the youngest grad student at MIT, and to say other students resent me for it is an understatement. To top it all off, I miss my Stunner. He's been with me through the darkest moments of my life, helping me pull myself back together. He's seen me at my worst -- I want him to see me at my best. If he'd just return my calls, I might be able to get myself around the mean girls (and boys) at school.

Stunner -- To say I've got skeletons in my closet is the understatement of the century. Suzie deserves a man more suited to her station than me, and she definitely deserves a man who's not a stone-cold killer. I have my uses. Protecting her body, heart, and soul is one of those. I just never expected to fall for the woman after the girl grew up.

Now not only has she run into a foul and vindictive bastard, my past has caught up to me, and there may be no way to keep from being swept back up into the madness. All I truly know is I won't let any of it touch Suzie -- even if it means giving her up. Forever.

Chapter One

"You staying here during break again?" The svelte redhead, Rebecca Tillerson, was not Suzie's favorite person. As a rule, all the graduate students at MIT thought Suzie was weird because she didn't socialize with anyone. More than one of the people living in her graduate housing openly made fun of her. Intellectually, Suzie knew they were threatened by her. She was the youngest person currently in a graduate program and had proven invaluable in helping her professors get funding for major projects both inside and outside her major of Astronautics and Aeronautics. More than one of the math professors routinely snagged her outside normal channels, and it had ruffled feathers of many of the math grad students.

"Haven't decided," Suzie answered. "Depends on my family's schedule."

Rebecca laughed merrily. "You say that like your family has all kinds of important things to do. You come from a hick town in Kentucky. What could they possibly be doing?"

"Well, my dad owns a security company. Sometimes he has to go to headquarters in South Carolina. I don't like going because of the soldiers there. They're kind of scary." As always, Suzie talked too much.

Rebecca's eyes got wide. "Scary? You mean you don't go and hook up with one of the security guys? Even for the evening?"

"I don't like scary men," Suzie said softly.

The other woman's mockery made Suzie's face flame. "You've got to be kidding me! You're an even bigger wuss than I thought." Rebecca looked up at a busty blonde woman approaching them. "Georgina!

You've got to hear this!" She looked back at Suzie, amused contempt in her gaze. "What's the name of this security company your dad supposedly owns?"

Suzie really wanted to just leave, to turn her nose up at the two women and get the hell out. Instead, she found herself answering. Just like she always did when the two women berated and humiliated her. "ExFil Corporation."

Rebecca snorted. "Your dad doesn't own that place. It's some service guy who's a biker or something. Real badass."

"He does. Joe Gill is my dad, and he owns ExFil."

"Whatever. Georgina, little miss thang over here doesn't like 'scary men.'" She made air quotes. "That's why she doesn't go home during breaks. Because if her dad has to go to ExFil headquarters, she's afraid to be around them."

Georgina looked at Suzie like she was crazy. "You mean all those muscled, crazy-hot guys don't do it for you?" She gave a disbelieving snicker. "You're too much, Suzie. Stick to math. You're good at that. But you're a horrible liar."

"I'm not lying!" She didn't know why she felt the need to defend herself because, no matter what she said, Georgina and Rebecca would never believe her when they were wanting to make fun of her.

"Oh, please! You're telling us that your dad owns the biggest security firm in North America and yet you're going to college? If he were that loaded, you'd be home, basking in the sun and waiting on your inheritance. You aren't rich. You're just some freak of nature who wants people to believe she's something."

"I've got classes to prepare for," Suzie muttered, and headed up to her apartment. To her utter embarrassment, the two women laughed so loudly there was no way everyone in the stupid building hadn't heard.

College sucked. Like royally sucked *ass*. Suzie tried to spend most of her days either in the library or the computer lab. The parts of her days she had to actually attend a class or a practicum, she usually kept her head down and did just what she had to in order to scrape by. Being with others wasn't her favorite thing. She'd rather be back home with Bones.

Bones was a motorcycle club she and the two boys who'd protected her during a dark time in her life had stumbled onto and basically moved in with. The man who had adopted her, Joe Gill, aka Cain, was the club's president. Cain and Angel had adopted all three of them. How, Suzie had no idea, but no one had come looking for them, Social Services had only visited once, and the next thing they all knew, they were Cliff, Daniel, and Suzie Gill.

Suzie wasn't naive enough to think Cliff and Daniel had actually stumbled onto the only club across God only knew how many states who would take responsibility for three teenagers, but she didn't look too closely at it. Most likely Daniel had found them by snooping in places he shouldn't. Being sneaky was his talent. Cliff and Daniel were both three or four years older than she was, but they'd done their best to protect her even though it meant things were always harder on them. For that, she'd never be able to repay them. As she'd gotten older and ventured from her safe haven of the clubhouse, she'd realized what they must have gone through.

Suzie tried not to think about any of that if she could help it. Unfortunately, Igg and Ook downstairs made her go back to those dark days after she'd been taken. She sighed as she stepped off the elevator to her floor. No way she could avoid the nightmares tonight.

Currently, her most pressing problem was the coming fall break. She desperately wanted to go back home to Kentucky. The only problem was she didn't drive, and she refused to ask Cain or anyone else at Bones for more money or to take time out of their schedule to look after her even more than they already had. They'd gone out on a limb to pay her tuition for her until she could get a job and pay them back. MIT didn't give scholarships on merit. They gave financial aid based on income. Because she was unwilling to draw attention to herself even now over her family status, she'd had to do some creative accounting to fudge tax documents and, in the end, had made it sound impossible for her to get aid for college.

She'd actually hoped that would be the end of the MIT journey, but Cain had insisted she was going if she got in, and had paid the full tuition price. Owning one of the top security companies in the world, he'd said it was no problem. She didn't believe that, and, even if it were true, she didn't deserve to take his money. She only went because he insisted and Suzie owed him and Angel. Big time.

The prospect of staying at school during fall break stressed her out and made her sad for more than one reason. Sure, she missed her family, and, really, every single member of Bones -- patched member or prospect -- was her family, but more than anything she missed Stunner.

From the first day she'd come to live with Cain, Stunner had been there watching over her. Her own personal very large, very strong, very protective security blanket. He was more than a protector and best friend though. No matter what she tried to tell herself, or what she wanted other people to believe, she was in love with the brooding man. Had been since he'd forced his way into her life and refused to be separated from her for a very long time afterward. Well, until Angel had talked her into going to MIT. Suzie hadn't even been serious about it. She'd just applied on a whim after completing a mathematics BS online. It had seemed ludicrous at the time. Why in the world would MIT take a student who'd graduated from an online program, no matter that it had been Purdue through their Global University program. Right?

But they had. Then Angel found out, and Suzie absolutely would not disappoint her mother. Not ever. Surprisingly, Stunner hadn't protested. He'd been restless the week leading up to her departure, but he hadn't gone with them to take her to MIT, and she only saw him when she went home. This was her first year there, and she hadn't been home in weeks. Which meant she missed Stunner like she might miss her right hand.

She'd texted him a few times, but he always responded with one-word answers or an emoji or something. Calling was even worse because he wasn't much for conversations. And she couldn't bring herself to admit she loved him.

But after this latest run-in with Rebecca, she needed him.

Once inside her apartment, she clicked the lock and turned the deadbolt. The chain was next. Safely locked inside, she went to her bedroom and grabbed the blanket Stunner had always wrapped her in when she was younger and needed him to hold her when the nightmares got too bad, and crawled into the closet. She sat back in the far corner behind some boxes. It was a little nest in a cubby hole she'd made the first night she'd arrived. There were pillows and blankets in case she felt the need to stay in there for longer than a few minutes. Leaning out of her hiding place, she pulled the door closed, then huddled under her blanket and cried until she fell asleep.

* * *

"FIGHT!"

Stunner bared his teeth at Pig. The fucking bastard had opened his fucking mouth for the last fucking time. The alarm had been sounded the second Pig had uttered the words "girl's a fuckin' pussy," in reference to Suzie and how she avoided the Boneyard when she was home.

The call to arms went out over the bar from the recently patched member, Kickstand. Despite being friends with Pig, Kickstand had turned out to be a loyal member of Bones and a good guy if a little shy in the brains department. Like how he continued to be friends with this motherfucker.

Good thing the warning had gone out, because Stunner had had all he was taking from the stupid pissant. Stunner was out of his chair and had the former prospect for Bones by the throat. By the time everyone realized where the fight was, Stunner had slammed Pig against the wall three times, not taking care with his head. If he beat the fucker to death, he'd get rid of the body where no one would ever find it.

"Back the fuck off, Stunner!" Bohannon, the club's enforcer, tried to pry Stunner's fingers from around Pig's throat. Stunner didn't take his eyes from Pig's. If he killed the man, he was going to look into his eyes while he did it. He stopped beating Pig's head against the wall, but only because it was wood and gave just enough to prevent him from splitting the other man's skull. So he resorted to squeezing the life out of him. Less mess that way. Not like anyone would miss the fucker. The club had been trying to get rid of him for a couple of years now. This seemed like as good a time as any.

"I know we want rid of him, Stunner, but not like this! We don't kill without a good reason." Bohannon was still freeing Pig from Stunner. "Let him go!"

Had he spoken out loud? Just as well. If they knew his intention, they could get anyone out of the bar who wasn't Bones, and he could finish this business where he should have started it. In private.

"He's gonna kill the fucker this time." That was Kickstand. Kid sounded distressed. Like Stunner gave a good Goddamn. If the kid was stupid enough to think Pig was worth saving, he deserved the heartache. "I tried to tell him to back off, Cain. Told him he didn't want to poke Stunner, but he wouldn't listen."

"Stunner!"

Stunner turned to look at the Bones president. Unable to stop himself, he growled at the other man. No way he was taking away his kill. Not this time. Cain raised an eyebrow and glanced at someone beside him.

"Don't look at me. He might be my sister's kid, but I've been thinkin' 'bout killin' the stupid cunt my own damned self."

"Well, he can't do it here, Arkham," Cain said, sounding annoyed. "Not with half the bar seein' the start of the fuckin' fight."

Arkham sighed. "Fine. But this happens again, you're on your own."

All that registered in the back of Stunner's mind, but his real focus was on watching Pig slowly lose consciousness. It wouldn't be long after that until he died. Satisfaction filled Stunner, and he took a deep breath, relishing the thought. He was going to choke the life out of the fucker.

Pig's face was now a satisfying shade of purple, and Stunner thought he might just finish the job before Cain could get enough people together to pull him off. Next thing he knew, several hands tugged at him and arms wrapped around him, pulling him off his prey. One fucker had his arm around Stunner's neck, but he wasn't concerned about someone choking him. He was pissed he might miss the moment Pig died. No way that was happening.

"No!" Stunner was desperate to hang on to Pig. They'd have to pry his fingers off the fucker's neck. After they cut off his arm, Goddammit. There was no way he was letting go voluntarily.

"What the fuck did Pig say to set Stunner off like this?" Cain sounded equal parts pissed and exasperated. There might have been a touch of worry in there for some fucking reason.

"Get Stunner off him and the two of you go across the room," Kickstand said. "Then I'll think about tellin' ya."

"Stunner, let that fucker go, NOW!" Cain's voice was hard with authority. Normally, Stunner would have done what the president told him immediately when he used that voice. Hell, he'd only ever heard it a couple of times since he'd been with Bones, and it had made him cringe even when it wasn't directed at him. Now, though, well. It was going to take more than a true hardass to keep him from making this kill. Not even Cain was going to stop this.

Finally, someone managed to pry his fingers from Pig's throat. Stunner let out a war bellow that promised retaliation. He knew he wasn't thinking clearly, knew he needed to take a step back and get himself under control, but he couldn't. He couldn't think beyond the rage and longing, and emptiness, and loneliness that filled him. In his heart, he knew that, if he killed Pig now it would somehow make him worthy. Of *her*. Becoming worthy in her eyes was worth any amount of pain later. And Lord knew Cain would dish out the pain if Stunner openly disobeyed him.

"Back the fuck off, Stunner," Cain said again, getting between him and Pig. Stunner tried to look around the other man, to get a bead on Pig so he could see the best way back to him to finish the job. "Look at me! Eyes on me!"

Reluctantly, Stunner shook his head, knowing Cain wasn't going to let him kill Pig. Not tonight. He closed his eyes and took a deep breath, leashing the madness inside him.

"Eyes on me," Cain said again. He sounded calmer this time. Not the hardass Stunner knew him to be. "You back with me?"

Stunner paused for several seconds. Was he? Yeah. He had it under control. Unfortunately. He gave a short nod and stood straighter, no longer ready to attack.

"Good. Now, you go sit." Cain pointed to a corner table. One where he could sit with his back to the wall and see the entire room and anyone coming or going. It happened on occasion that someone had a PTSD flashback, and Cain had prepared for it. If he was able to get that person back in control, he had a place for them to sit and breathe through it or talk to someone, or just fucking sit and drink coffee or ice water until they were ready to leave. Stunner suspected Cain knew this wasn't PTSD for him, but if he didn't ask, Stunner wouldn't tell him. Which was probably not going to happen. Cain would demand to know why Stunner had nearly killed someone in the club's bar.

The place was called the Boneyard, and it drew bikers from all over the region. At any given time, it was packed. Tonight was no exception, though it was getting late, and when the fight had started, most had either left on their own or had been encouraged to leave. Given the fact that Stunner was one big motherfucker, all but the true hardasses had left, fearful that he might turn on someone else. Fights weren't unusual, but they weren't always this serious.

Once Arkham had hoisted Pig over his shoulder and left with him and Kickstand, Cain kicked everyone else out but Pops and snagged a beer from the bar. He sat across the table from Stunner and offered him the bottle.

"Wanna tell me why you nearly popped Pig's head like a fuckin' tick?"

"No," Stunner growled, taking a long pull from the bottle.

"Tough shit. Tell me anyway."

Stunner met Cain's gaze for long moments. Did he tell Cain what Pig had said? If he did, would Cain see through him? Would he finally know?

"Stop fuckin' stalling, Stunner." Cain scrubbed a hand over his face. "I need to get home. Angel's fretting over if she's going to just drive up to Cambridge and drag Suzie home or wait for her to call and tell her what plans she has."

Immediately Stunner sat up straighter. "Suzie's comin' home? She OK?"

"She's fine, Stunner." Cain gave him a quizzical look. "Haven't you talked to her?"

Stunner grunted. "Couple of times."

"Just tell me what happened."

Yeah. He wasn't getting out of this one. "He insulted her."

Cain narrowed his eyes and shook his head. "Who insulted who?"

"Pig. He insulted Suzie."

Silence.

"OK. I can see how that might upset you. You've been her best friend for a very long time." When Stunner offered nothing, Cain dropped his arms to the table in an exasperated motion. "So? What'd he say?"

Stunner sighed. Surrender was sometimes the better part of valor. Or some shit. "He implied Suzie was a coward 'cause she don't like to be around crowds."

Cain's expression went instantly hard. "Those his exact words?"

Stunner shrugged.

Again, when Stunner offered nothing else, Cain prompted him. From the look and sound of him, Cain was rapidly losing his patience with Stunner. "So? What'd he fuckin' say?"

"He called her…" Stunner cleared his throat, tilting his head as if he were the one choking. "He said she was a fuckin' pussy who wasn't worth a shit for nothin'."

Cain had his cell out and was texting one-handed as he stood, knocking the chair over backward in his haste. Naturally, Stunner followed. Without a word Cain stalked out to the parking lot where Arkham had a slightly groggy Pig half sitting against Arkham's bike seat. Arkham had just pulled out his cell and looked back to the door of the Boneyard. Whatever Arkham saw in Cain's face made him raise his hands in surrender and back away. Pig glanced up, saw Cain coming for him, and immediately knew he was in trouble.

He proceeded to squeal like his namesake.

No one in the parking lot stood in Cain's way. Even Arkham stood back, though Stunner got the feeling Arkham thought this saved him from having to beat Pig himself. It was apparent someone had to do it. But, Goddammit, Stunner wanted to! Cain, as president, had the final say in everything to do with Bones. He usually weighed the others' opinions very carefully, but this was completely on him. Suzie was, after all, Cain's daughter, if not by birth, certainly of the heart. At this point, the only person who was going to save Pig's life was Angel. And she wasn't there.

Stunner had mixed emotions as Cain threw the first punch. The sound of flesh meeting flesh was loud, even in the open parking lot. Surprisingly, no one said a word. Not of encouragement. Not for Cain to stop. Instead, to Stunner, it seemed like they were bearing witness to a punishment. One Pig might not survive, and no one really cared. They trusted Cain to do what needed doing.

Pig begged and screamed over and over. Each time Cain punched or kicked the other man, Stunner grew more and more disgruntled. He needed the violence to release some of the tension inside him. Besides, Suzie was his to defend, dammit!

Just as Stunner realized Pig was unconscious, a bike pulled onto the gravel parking lot of the Boneyard and Angel jumped off the back as best she could, headed toward Cain at a dead run. A quick glance, and Stunner saw that Shadow had brought her to the bar.

"Cain!" She called. "Cain, stop! Please!"

Heaving, blood splattered up his arms and over his face, Cain obeyed his tiny wife. He was a better man than Stunner was. Even if Suzie had begged him to stop, he wasn't sure he could have pulled himself off Pig. The man had tormented Suzie from the day she'd set foot on the place. Stunner had watched it and discouraged Pig many times. But it wasn't until the Christmas when Pig had berated her for decorating and putting glitter in Stunner's beard that he'd finally snapped. He'd beaten the kid to within an inch of his life that day. Right in front of Suzie. She should have been terrified of Stunner, but she'd allied herself even more closely. He'd done the same with her.

After that first beating, Pig had pretty much steered clear of Suzie when Stunner was around. But sometimes, especially after he'd been drinking, the man lost his Goddamned mind.

Instead of acknowledging his wife, Cain turned to Arkham, pointing a finger at the other man. "I don't fuckin' care if he's related to you. Get him gone or the next time he does or says anything remotely disparaging to or about Suzie, I'll fuckin' kill the little cunt where he stands."

No one was watching Pig or paying attention to Stunner. Everyone had turned to Cain and Arkham, waiting for instructions. Because there would be instructions. Probably from Arkham, telling them where to dump Pig. Stunner used that time to advance on Pig and grab him by his collar, intending to drag him off into the woods and finish the job.

"Stop!" That was Cain. Man didn't miss much. Stunner kept hold of Pig but looked back over his shoulder at the Bones president, not saying a word. "You ain't killin' him this time, Stunner."

Every muscle in Stunner's body tensed. He wanted to bare his teeth and growl. He'd already been denied a kill once, and he had no desire to be denied a second time.

"Stunner," Angel said, pulling away from Cain and going to Stunner. "Please do what Cain says." She looked so filled with anguish Cain couldn't possibly deny her. He *wanted* to, but just couldn't.

"He's not a good person, ma'am," he murmured. "Suzie doesn't deserve to have him talking about her like he does. He doesn't do it where you or Cain can hear. Most of the time he doesn't do it where I can hear. But Suzie hears. Ain't havin' him be mean to her."

"I know, Stunner. And I appreciate you protecting her like this. You have no idea how much. She loves you like a brother. Probably more than she loves me and Cain or Cliff and Daniel. I don't want you killing. Not like this. I know you can take care of yourself, but it still worries me. And Suzie? If you get rid of Pig and Cain's people can't cover up the killing, you'll be put away, and Suzie would be devastated. I won't have that for her. She tries to be strong and in many ways, she is. But inside her heart, she's fragile. I'm not certain she'd survive it if you left her to go to prison."

Just like that, Stunner's heart plummeted. Not only because he couldn't kill Pig, but because he was destined to cause Suzie pain no matter what he did now or in the future. If the only way he could be worthy for Suzie to be his was to kill her tormentor, then he was royally fucked. Because now he couldn't kill Pig any more than he could outrun his past. His past would catch up to him one day, and he'd hurt her no matter what role he played in her life, for two reasons. One, he'd already killed. *So fucking many times.* He'd killed until he'd thought he was dead inside. Two, if Cain knew the extent of his past and who it was linked to and why he'd come to Bones to begin with, Cain would kill him. And Stunner wouldn't lift a finger to stop him.

No. Better he let Suzie be. She was starting a new life for herself at one of the best universities in the country. The best thing he could do was to stay away from her.

Giving Angel a sharp nod, he dropped Pig and strode to his bike. He kept his shoulders back and his head up. He didn't look at anyone and did his best to keep his expression neutral. Inside, though, he was raging. His heart was breaking into tiny pieces at what he'd lost before he'd even known he wanted her. With a quick kick of the starter, Stunner put his Harley in gear and took off, racing into the setting sun. If he was lucky, maybe he could hurl the nightmares into the fiery ball before they could take hold of him once again.

Chapter Two

Suzie lay on the small couch in her apartment staring at the computer chat screen. She'd debated whether or not to call her parents all afternoon. Everyone in the building was gone. She was the only holdout. She'd thought most of the grad students would want to take advantage of the lab space and vacant library to work, but she'd been wrong. Maybe they were just trying to get away from her. More than one of them had referred to her as "Little Miss Goodie Two Shoes" on more than one occasion. Also among the insults were brown noser, suck up, kiss ass, and several other things she just ignored. It wasn't her fault she'd rather work than hang out with people she didn't know in bars that weren't nearly as safe as the Boneyard. Maybe she *was* a wimp.

Finally, unable to take the isolation a moment longer, she pulled up her mother's name from the contact selection. It took several seconds but Angel answered the call, Cain right beside her.

"Hi, sweetheart!" Angel's eyes were bright and excited and so full of love Suzie had to blink several times to keep the tears at bay.

"Hi, Mom. I miss you guys!"

"We miss you too, honey," Cain said, his smile warm and engaging. When Suzie had first met the man, she hadn't thought him capable of such a look. He was so hard and rough, but he was a protector through and through. That meant he protected her physically as well as emotionally. Which meant he'd learned to genuinely smile on occasion. For her and Angel. "How's school?"

She tried to keep the uncertainty out of her expression and her voice. "It's OK. Taking some getting used to. It might be MIT, but people are mostly interested in partying."

Angel gave her a puzzled look. "And you're not?"

"Not really. I've got several projects going on and classes to teach. It's hard to keep up with all of it."

Cain immediately took up the camera. "If you're not ready for this, Suzie, I'll come get you."

"No! It's not that! I love the work. The more I do, the more the professors put on me. I think they like that I follow through. I'm actually doing more math-related classes than astronautics." She smiled brightly. "But math makes the world go 'round."

Angel giggled. "It certainly does, baby." There was a small pause as Angel glanced up at Cain. Her dad was about to say something, but Angel interrupted him. "So, you wanting to come home for Fall Break?" The question was asked casually, but Suzie could tell her mother wanted her to come home. Suzie did, too.

"No. I have a lot of work to do. I just wanted to touch base with everyone. How's Cliff and Daniel?" It was a deflection. She could tell Cain saw it, but Angel just wiped her eyes once and plowed on.

"They're good. Both are coming home next weekend and starting their training with Cain, Bohannon, and Sword." Angel beamed, obviously proud of the boys, but mostly just glad they were coming home.

"They do well enough, I'll hire them at ExFil." Cain looked even more proud than Angel.

"What about Hannah and Gunnar? They managed a takeover yet?" Suzie was still deflecting, but, like everyone else in the club, she loved the little ones more than life itself. When she was home, she spent most of her time with the babies, especially

Willa, Helen and Trucker's baby. She was surprised none of the other ol' ladies had children yet, but she knew most of them were now actively trying. They all giggled about it -- and the fun in trying -- every time they got together.

Cain laughed. "Not yet, but it was touch and go for a while. I actually expect Hannah to break off and start her own chapter soon. Might even start an offshoot of ExFil."

"That sounds about right," Suzie agreed, smiling affectionately.

"They're definitely positioning themselves for either that or a hostile takeover," Angel added. "Could be either."

Again, there was a silence, her parents still smiling but looking at her expectantly. Finally, she took a breath, careful to keep her smile in place. "Stunner wouldn't happen to be around, would he?"

Angel looked up at Cain, her smile faltering. Cain's grin remained firmly in place, but Suzie knew enough to see the strain and worry in his eyes. "He's fine. Had a small scuffle last night but walked away without a scratch."

Suzie knew her dad well. He was telling her the strict truth, but was holding back more than he wanted her to know. If she pushed, they might figure out her interest in Stunner was more than that of a treasured friend. If she didn't, she'd worry herself into a panic attack.

"I-I tried to call him, but he wasn't answering his phone."

Angel gasped slightly, and Cain turned the camera away from her, moving a little distance away so Suzie couldn't see her mother. "He's probably got a lot on his mind, baby. Don't take it personal. He'll see you called and get back with you."

"What's going on?" No way she could keep herself from asking. Something was way wrong, and her heart sped up, her mind going in a thousand different directions. Most prevalent was the question as to if there was a woman involved.

"Pig showed up at the Boneyard last night with Kickstand. Pig and Stunner got into a bit of a scuffle. You know how Stunner hates Pig. Anyway, I finished it. Pig won't be back, Kickstand is on probation, and Stunner decided he needed some space."

Suzie felt the blood drain from her face. "Where'd he go?"

"Didn't say. I suspect he's on his way to Palm Beach. Got a call from Thorn this morning asking if everything was good. Stunner probably reached out to them as a courtesy. Thorn finally got the deal closed on that old firehouse he wanted to buy a few months ago. They're moving the club, and Stunner will be a big help to them in the muscle department."

"H-he went to Florida?"

Cain frowned. "Yeah, baby. But he'll still be there if you need him."

Suzie wasn't so sure. Stunner had barely spoken to her since she started MIT. Had he decided she was grown up enough he could finally get on with his life? That she didn't need his protection anymore?

"O-OK. Just…" She took a breath. "If you talk to him, tell him to call me?"

"You got it, sweetheart."

She gave everyone her love and made them promise to hug and kiss all the babies for her. The second she could, Suzie signed off and took several deep breaths.

Immediately, she clicked Stunner's profile icon and clicked the "call" button. It rang several times. No answer. She picked up her cell and called him. Again, no answer. She tried again. Same result. The third time, it went straight to voicemail. Suzie felt like she'd been gutted. That was deliberate. He'd turned his phone off. He was avoiding her. Last thing she did was send off a text.

Whatever I did, I'm sorry.

Tears rolled down her cheeks unchecked. Her mind was in chaos. Her heart in shreds.

Stunner… *was gone.*

* * *

Suzie's text made Stunner want to howl in anguish. He'd just pulled into Salvation's Bane's new compound when he'd gotten the text. He'd known she'd called, but, being on the road, couldn't answer. Sure, he had a Bluetooth earpiece and mic hooked to his phone, but it was still hard to hear with the wind and the noise of the pipes.

On the other hand, he *had* been avoiding her. At first because he missed her so much he wasn't certain he could hold himself together. If he lost it, he was liable to drive his ass to Cambridge, throw Suzie over his shoulder, and carry her sweet ass home. That would sure make school comfortable for her. She'd hate him, and rightly so. Then the whole thing with Pig had happened, and he knew Angel's feelings about the whole situation. She and Cain expected Stunner to be Suzie's best friend. Nothing more. He couldn't blame them for it, because he knew he was nothing but trouble. Had been since he was thirteen.

But the pain in those five words in that text…

He could practically see the tears in her lovely eyes, streaking down her pale cheeks. Caused by him.

His immediate reaction was to call her. Fuck, to *get to her*. But he doubted he'd fit in on any fancy college campus. He was a scruffy, rough biker. He doubted anyone at MIT looked like he did.

Stunner resisted the urge to text her back. For about five seconds.

Sry. Ridin.

There. That would satisfy her. And keep him from having to interact with her.

She didn't text back. At first, he was relieved. His blowing her off had discouraged her from continuing to call or text. But when she hadn't called back that night, or the next day, he realized he was going to have to make the first move. Because he was a fucking idiot.

* * *

"Stunner!" Vicious, of Salvation's Bane, called to him across the common room. As with Bones, that was where they all hung out when not working or riding. It doubled as a party room, and there was a party planned that night. Shadow, a man he'd prospected with and taken his oath as a patched member of Bones alongside, had told him once that he needed to get laid. Desperately. Stunner had planned on it tonight. The party would have plenty of women to choose from, and all of them willing and eager to fuck the biggest, baddest biker among them. Stunner qualified on all counts. "Cain called. Asked you to give him a call when you got the chance."

Fuck. Cain had to have known calling Stunner's cell would get him nowhere. Instead of swearing out loud, however, Stunner nodded at Vicious, acknowledging the man without actually agreeing to anything. Not that he'd ignore his president.

With a sigh, he took out his phone and stabbed Cain's name. His president picked up on the first ring.

"You talked to Suzie lately?"

"No."

When there was no answer, Cain sighed. "I know you ain't big on talkin' much, brother, but I need you to this time."

"Ain't talked to 'er. Texted 'er when I first got here."

"When was that?"

"Yesterday."

That seemed to satisfy Cain. "Good. She was anxious to talk to you. I think she misses you."

He grunted, not saying more.

"Well, since you've been in touch with her… Good. That's all I wanted." Cain sounded like he wanted to say more, but was hesitating. Stunner knew the man well enough to not hang up the phone. He wanted to, but didn't want the other man disappointed in him.

"You tell her about your fight?"

"No."

"Well, I did. You need to talk to her, Stunner."

Stunner winced. He didn't want to talk to her about that. Angel had already let her feelings be known about Suzie and him, and Cain hadn't indicated he felt any differently about Stunner dating his daughter.

"She'll be fine. Best I just leave it at that."

Again, silence.

"Wait." Stunner could all but hear Cain narrowing his eyes as he worked out everything Stunner refused to say. It was one of the reasons Stunner didn't talk much. He'd learned early on in life that people could read a lot into a person's words. Even things best kept hidden. That was especially true around Cain. "This was more than Pig insulting Suzie.

Wasn't it?" When Stunner still didn't say anything -- what *could* he say? -- Cain sighed. "Goddammit, Stunner. I can't help if you don't tell me what the fuck's going on."

"Nothin' goin' on. If Suzie needs me, you know where to find me."

"Yeah. But does she?"

"You didn't tell her?" He knew Cain would have told Suzie where he was. He was just calling out the other man, reminding him that, despite what everyone thought, Stunner wasn't stupid.

"You know I did," Cain snapped. "And stop trying to deflect. This is about you and Suzie…" Cain trailed off. "You…" Stunner heard Cain's indrawn breath. "And Suzie?"

"No," was all Stunner said. There was no "him and Suzie." Not in the way Cain thought.

"But you want it that way."

"No."

"Fuck! Stunner, just… Goddamn! Would you stop being so fuckin' closed mouthed? Fuckin' talk to me!"

"Nothin' to talk about."

"If this is about what Angel said, she had no idea you felt that way about Suzie. You know neither of us would be against you testing the waters with her. Hell, that girl hasn't looked at you like a brother in a long fuckin' time. I know for Goddamned sure you're the best person in the fuckin' world to protect her." Cain was silent for a while. "You know, Stunner, this is hurting her."

Yeah. He got that.

"You need to talk to her. Figure out what she wants and see if it's what you want."

"You orderin' me to come back home?"

"No. Ain't no one can make this decision for you. You do what you feel like you need to do. I just hope you know what you're fuckin' doin'."

Stunner thought about staying silent, but he owed Cain more than the other man knew. An explanation on this didn't seem too much to give. He'd never tell Cain all of it, but he'd at least give him something.

"Angel's right. Suzie don't need a killer in her life, Cain. I'm a killer. Have been since I was thirteen. Don't want my past to touch her. Kept it all a secret and hid. But we both know a man can only run so long. Past'll catch up with me someday, and Suzie would be the collateral damage."

Cain was silent for so long, Stunner thought he might have finally gotten his point across. Then Cain spoke again. "We all have pasts, man. Every fuckin' one of us. And we've all killed. You have something hangin' over you, all you gotta do is tell me. It'll be taken care of."

"I ain't the man for her, Cain. But I'll find a way to always watch over her."

"I can do that my own Goddamned self!" Cain snapped. "She's my daughter. *She's your woman!* Fuckin' treat her like it!" The call ended.

Goddamned motherfuck! Stunner threw his cell phone across the room. Straight into a freshly plastered wall. It left a hole, but, thankfully, didn't shatter the phone. Now he had a hole to patch.

"Hope everything's OK," Beast said as he walked into the room. "'Cause if it's not and you start makin' holes in the wall me and Havoc just finished, you might find yourself headed back to Kentucky a helluva lot sooner than expected."

Stunner grunted, scrubbing his hand over his face. Then he did something he never thought he'd do. "I need help."

Chapter Three

"I need you to take over the Complex Variables class, Suzie. I've got to help Dr. Fresno with his rocket project." The man demanding she take over the math class was not her boss. In fact, he wasn't even in the same Masters program she was in. Jake Salisberry was a mathematics major, and not a very good one. In fact, there were rumors the only reason he was in the graduate program at all was because someone on the university's board of directors owed his daddy a favor. Suzie had been so out of sorts since the fall break fiasco she felt like she was riding a razor's edge between violence and tears. At the moment, she was leaning toward violence.

"Seems to me, being the Astronautics and Aeronautics grad student, I'd be more qualified than you to work on that project." Suzie didn't look up from the paper she was grading. "In fact, given you're a mathematics major, you should be teaching all the math classes you've had me doing so you can participate in fun projects you're not remotely qualified for, or are any good at."

She always set up her workstation in the library on Mondays and Wednesdays and the Math Lab on Tuesdays and Thursdays. Part of her graduate work included tutoring, and she liked to make sure undergraduates could find her no matter their major. Despite what her fellow grad students thought of her, the undergrads took advantage of her brain when they could. Her tutoring schedule was always full and, when someone couldn't get an appointment, they sought her out in the afternoon and evenings when she graded papers. Today was Friday so she sat at one of the many desks in the graduate dorm lobby. She considered it the last avenue for a student needing help. If they missed her through the week, they had two hours in the afternoon to catch her before the weekend.

For long moments, Suzie thought Jake would keep his mouth shut and move on. She didn't dare look up. Doing that would be the equivalent of flinching. If she flinched, he'd be all over her.

"What did you say to me?"

Suzie kept her focus on her work even though she couldn't process anything on the page. "I don't think I stuttered. You want free of your Complex Variables class, I suggest you talk to your supervising professor. If he requests my services, he should talk to mine." This was really unlike Suzie, so it was understandable if it threw Jake off. Also understandable if he rallied quickly and came at her again. Which he did.

"Who do you think you are? Do you have any idea who my father is?"

"Not really, and, quite frankly I couldn't care less." She finally looked up at him, careful to keep her expression one of boredom. "Now, if you'll excuse me, I'm really busy, and I think there are undergrads waiting for me."

"You little cunt! I suggest you do what I tell you to or you might just be sorry. My father owns half the state and has every board member at this university in his pocket. He'll get you expelled before you can blink."

OK, that got her full attention. She placed her pencil on the desk and stood. Suzie remembered how her father looked when he was supremely displeased. She remembered how scary he could look. She went for that look now.

"I've been called that name for the last fucking time," she said, keeping her voice soft and deadly like her father could do. "Do your worst, you little fuck. My daddy's meaner than your daddy. And I bet my daddy carries a bigger fucking gun."

That brought Jake up short. He didn't really know what to say, but his face turned every shade of red she could have possibly imagined. He looked around, making sure no one could see or hear. They were in a public place, but no one was near enough that he felt the need to mind his language. Or his words.

Jake bent to place his palms on her desk. "You'll regret this. I know where you live." He gave her a grin evil enough to give her chill bumps. "If you think you're the first little cunt I've had to put in her place, well, you're not." He stood, still grinning. "I'll be seeing you around."

"Looking fucking forward to it," she said, dismissively. She picked up her pencil and went back to her papers, trying her best to control her breathing and the shaking of her hands.

"Suzie?"

Her head snapped up. Jake had started to leave the building when the man who'd spoken passed him. Jake turned to watch, mouth agape, as the biggest man Suzie had ever seen walked through the door. She thought she'd known the voice, but the visual was someone she didn't recognize. But she knew the set of the man's shoulders. The piercing blue eyes so cold they could freeze blood in the veins of an enemy. She even knew the hesitant gait as he approached her. And how did the body she remembered look so much bigger than the last time she'd seen him?

"I -- S-Stunner?"

The man before her was dressed in a crisp suit with a cleanly shaven face and an expensive haircut. The suit he wore was tailored perfectly to his broad shoulders, muscular arms and thighs, and narrow waist. He looked like something out of *GQ*, not *Biker Weekly*.

"Yeah," he said, then corrected himself. "Yes." His hand went nervously to the silk tie at his throat to adjust it. He just stopped himself and glanced at his watch instead. Another expensive addition to his new wardrobe. "I, uh, that is, would you mind if we go somewhere more private? We need to talk."

That voice…

Stunner had this husky gravel when he spoke, like he was out of practice speaking. This man was smooth as honey, a deep rich baritone that could melt panties two states away. She had the thought that he had the voice of an angel he kept hidden and the voice of a demon he made sure everyone heard. Like he was given the choice of which voice he wanted, looked at his creator, and calmly said, "Yes."

"Your beard," she said inanely. "You shaved it?"

He shrugged. OK, *that* gesture she knew well. It was his way of deflecting without refusing to answer.

"Private," she said, her thoughts back to what he'd asked. "Yes. Let me just get my things." She gathered everything, placing them into two folders and closing her laptop. The second she started to pick them up, Stunner snatched everything and held it securely. He reached for her hand, which she took without hesitation.

"Who's that? We don't allow uninvited guests into this building, buddy," Jake said, looking Stunner up and down as if he were a bug he wanted to squish. *Yeah. Try it. Buddy.*

"This is my --"

"Fiancé," Stunner finished. "And you are?"

"Jake Salisberry," Suzie said, looking Jake straight in the eyes. "Jake, Stunner."

"What kind of name is Stunner?" Jake gave a cocky smirk, as if name calling and making fun of Stunner was going to make the big man slink off into the background.

"My call sign," Stunner said. "I'm special forces. Retired. Now I work for ExFil." He nodded to Suzie. "Her father, Cain, owns the security company." Stunner took a slow step toward Jake. "I've already beat the fuck outta the punk who called her a cunt before. If you think I didn't hear you, you're wrong." His voice had gone from that deep, pleasing tone to the gruff growl Suzie knew best. His demon voice. "I will beat a motherfucker down if I hear it happen again. No matter who your fuckin' daddy is. And no one will ever find your body."

Jake gave a little squeak and jumped back a step. The second he did, Suzie just happened to look down. A trickle of urine streamed down Jake's leg below the khaki shorts he wore. A dark, wet stain spread over his crotch, telling the tale of how bad Stunner had scared him.

Though she wanted to, Suzie said nothing acknowledging the man's dilemma. Instead, she pulled Stunner away with her small hand tucked into his big one. She was only willing to risk so much. "I have so much to talk to you about," she said, looking up at Stunner. She was truly happy to see him, but she was also hurt and angry. And why did he call himself her fiancé? Didn't that imply they'd at least be talking to each other? "Starting with, you know, your trip to Florida. Without me."

Surprisingly, Stunner winced. Where Jake hadn't cowed him in the least, her displeasure had him hanging his head like a naughty child. "I was only there a couple of days."

"And the haircut? And your *beard*? What am I gonna decorate come Christmas?" She got that out before they stepped into the elevator. It was really a discussion that should have happened in private, but the few people in the lobby were staring at Stunner, and her by extension. Most of them women. She wanted to let everyone on the whole fucking campus know who he was with. The second the elevator doors closed, she jerked her hand away, her anger and hurt finally pushing their way to the fore. "Don't touch me," she hissed.

He sighed, but didn't reach for her hand again. The second the doors opened, she shot out and hurried down the hall to her room. She unlocked the door and entered. It was small but neat. The only thing out of place was the quilt on the couch which lay in a heap at one end where she'd left it after her nap. The one where she'd cried herself to sleep because Stunner refused to talk to her.

"What are you doing here?" She approached him, reaching out to pick up the crisp lapel of his suit jacket. "And what the hell is this? Since when do you dress like this? Where's your colors?"

"I was trying to fit in on campus with you," he said. His voice was no longer smooth. He was back fully to the Stunner she knew. Well, except for the get-up. "Didn't want to embarrass you."

That melted her heart just a little. But she wasn't ready to let him off the hook. "Three days, Stunner. Three days since I last heard from you. Now you just waltz in here, pretending to be my boyfriend and... what? What was supposed to happen next?"

"You're upset."

"No! You think?" Even the sarcasm wasn't enough to keep the shaking at bay. Whether it was from anger over Stunner cutting her off, or fear because of the confrontation with Jake, or just pure relief to have him back, she had no idea. But she was doing her level best to hold onto her anger because she had a feeling she was going to need it.

"I can explain, if you'll let me." Coming from Stunner, that was huge. Explaining meant he'd have to use more than a couple of words at a time, possibly big words, and he was fond of neither. Not because he wasn't smart -- the man had a wickedly keen mind -- but because he had an aversion to talking for some reason. She always figured he'd tell her someday. Maybe this was it.

"Believe me, I'd love nothing more," she said, crossing her arms over her chest. "But not in that ridiculous outfit. Put on some jeans and a T-shirt. Then I'll see if I'm ready to listen to what you have to say."

He sighed. "I thought... I'd hoped you'd be pleased with my clothes and appearance."

"This isn't you, Stunner. At least, not the Stunner I know. Some blonde bimbo in Florida change all that?" Could she be any snippier? "Did the women of Salvation's Bane prove to be more than you had at home? More sophisticated and sexy? Did they take care of those manly needs all men seem to have?" She knew this was more than she had a right to throw at him. Given her past, it was downright cruel, but she couldn't stop the words and hurt and anger. She'd kept everything bottled up so tightly, only letting a little of it out when she realized he wasn't going to call her back, that there was simply no stopping the emotional explosion now.

"No, Suzie," he said, scrubbing a hand over his face like he was tired beyond description. "I'm sorry."

She sighed, a little deflated once the initial explosion was out. "No reason to be sorry. I'm in a bad mood and taking it out on you." She took the two steps separating them and wrapped her arms around his middle. "I've missed you so much." His arms came around her, holding her as tightly as she held him. "Don't mean I ain't kickin' your ass later though." She sniffed, aware she was crying and probably ruining his expensive suit.

He pulled away, sliding his hands up her arms and over her shoulders to cradle her face in his hands. He held her gaze for long moments, as if he was searching for something. Suzie simply stared back at him, knowing he'd get what he needed eventually. No amount of rushing him would help. In truth, she didn't want to rush him. The closer he was to her, the more he touched her and held her, the better she felt. Like a weight being lifted from her entire body. Finally, he nodded once, brushed a kiss over her forehead, then headed for the door.

"Where're you going?" Suzie's heart hammered. All the tension had drained from her while he'd been near. Now that crushing weight once again descended. He gave her a puzzled look, looking down at his clothes and picking at the crisp black button-up shirt. Hell, the man even had expensive-looking cufflinks. He'd gone all out, and she'd been less than impressed. *Way to go, Suzie.* "Oh." A flush of embarrassment flooded her. "Guess I did demand you change clothes."

He raised an eyebrow.

"I mean, if you didn't get more you'd be running around here naked. And you couldn't do that. Right?" Jesus! Did she sound like she *wanted* him naked in her apartment? "I didn't mean you should be naked." She twisted her fingers together, wringing her hands in her nerves. "I mean, unless you want to or something."

He barked out a laugh then. Without his beard, his smile was *devastating*. "I think you like the idea of me naked in here with you. But I'll only get naked if you will. Ain't barin' my soul unless you do."

Suzie sat down on the couch abruptly, her knees giving out so they were unable to hold her trembling body. Stunner shrugged out of his jacket, those piercing blue eyes seeming to penetrate her very soul. He stalked toward her as if she were his prey. In a way, she guessed she was. He'd obviously come here for her, but to what end? Was he serious about this fiancé business? Because she wasn't sure how she felt about it. Or, rather, how she *should* feel about it.

"You know I'd never hurt you, Suz. Right?" When she nodded, he grasped her chin in those strong fingers of his and tilted her head up to him, holding her still for his kiss.

It wasn't a deep or passionate kiss. More a gentle lingering, a moving over her mouth with his as he got a feel for her. His taste was like heaven. And what that simple touch did to her body? Well, Suzie was sexually innocent. Not so much in body -- Kiss of Death had taken care of that when she was eleven -- but in everything else. She had no clue what desire was supposed to feel like, but she was certain this was it.

She'd never even so much as looked at a porn video on the Internet, or even gone looking for images of people naked or having sex. She'd never read graphic romance novels, or romance novels at all, really. Anything to do with sex she'd shied away from, never wanting to relive that part of her life again. She saw how the men in Bones were with their women. No matter how young or old or their level of experience, the men were unfailingly kind and gentle. They pushed their women sexually sometimes, but never to the point of pain or humiliation. They'd all commented on it at different times.

Now, Suzie suspected that some of their talking about how their men treated them during sex might have been for her benefit. It had been their way of letting her know there were decent men out there who could help her with this in a caring, compassionate way, and maybe even show her things she'd never considered. Though she was still uncertain and more than a little frightened, she craved this. She wanted to experience what all her friends in Bones had experienced with their men. But only with Stunner.

When he lifted his head, he stroked her cheek as if to praise her for allowing him that much. "I'll always take care of you, Suz. No matter what you need, all you have to do is tell me and I'm there."

"Will you grow back your beard?" She reached up and stroked his smooth jaw with her fingers. "You don't look like yourself without it."

"Anything you want, baby. The boys at Bane thought I'd fit in better here with the clothes and fancy haircut. But if you want the beard back, I'll gladly grow it again."

She blinked. "I think this is the most you've said in one sitting since we met."

"Somethin' else I'm workin' on." He looked down, as if trying to decide on what to say. "A man once told me that the less you say, the less you give away. I learned a long time ago to only speak when strictly necessary."

"Well, you learned that lesson pretty well."

"I did. But for you, I'll do better. At least, when we're alone."

Suzie couldn't help the smile. This was a new side of Stunner she wanted to explore. "I'd like that."

He nodded once then turned to go again. Before he got to the door, he seemed to make a conscious effort to stop himself. He turned back to her. "I have a bag in the cage -- er -- car. I'll be right back."

As he shut the door behind him, Suzie actually giggled. She was still put out with him, but he'd gone a long way already toward making her feel better.

Chapter Four

Cain might well kill him. If not his president, his woman certainly would. This was going to happen. Suzie was his. Cain thought he knew what she needed, thought Stunner was a good man, but he was wrong on so many levels. He'd be loyal to her, protect her with everything in him down to his very life, but his needs ran dark. And she needed soft and sweet. Caring. Vanilla in the extreme. She needed someone who could show her the joys of sex and pleasure without pushing her too far. Stunner would definitely push her.

On his way out, he saw Jake on the phone. The man had changed his clothes and was really engrossed in his call, so much so he missed Stunner walking across the lobby. The second he did, Jake jumped up from his chair and put it between him and Stunner. Though he was hyperaware of the little fuck, Stunner merely glanced in his direction before turning away. He gave it just enough attention to let the other man know he was watching. He also knew Jake was doing his best to get Suzie in trouble. Most likely over Stunner being there. Which made him grind his teeth. Was the whole world conspiring against him? Was this even a good idea? If he got her kicked out of school, she'd never forgive him.

It was almost enough to make him get in the fucking cage and drive back to Florida with his tail tucked between his legs. Almost. Only the thought of Suzie waiting upstairs on him made him grab his duffle and head back to her.

Jake met him at the door. Yeah. Whole fucking world was against him.

"You don't belong here. And you certainly don't need a girl like Suzie. You do realize she's about to flunk out, right?"

Two women he'd noticed sitting in the corner watching him when he'd first entered the lobby approached him then. "Jake's right. Why not spend some time with real women? Not only are we smart, but we've got sex honed to a fine science."

The other one agreed with a wide, predatory smile. "We could definitely blow your mind." She glanced at his crotch. "Or other parts of your body."

"Not interested," he said without so much as a second glance. Turning to Jake he said, "Not sure what your problem with Suzie is, but this is the last time I talk to you."

When he started to go around the trio, Jake stepped in front of him, putting his hand in the middle of Stunner's chest to halt his progress. "You're obviously a man of means. You need a woman in your class. Obviously any woman at MIT would be better than someone like Suzie." He chuckled. "Hell, even her name is childish." He lowered his voice as if he were an old friend imparting the deal of a lifetime. "Look. My father knows people. He's not only an MIT graduate, but he's big in the field of weapons tech. Your ExFil operation probably got their weapons from him. He's making a deal with Argent Tech. Once it's complete, he'll be on their board. If you help me out here, I can see to it he'll help you out."

"With what?"

Jake looked at Stunner like he knew he had a sucker. Also, like he had Stunner right where he wanted him. Which was away from Suzie.

"With anything your boss needs. Look," he said when Stunner opened his mouth to answer. "Don't make any decisions until you talk with your boss. He'll be angry if you fuck up a good opportunity for him to save money. I might even get ExFil set up as a test facility."

Stunner wanted to point out that the son of a bitch had no idea what he was talking about. Instead he took out his cell -- a burner, so it didn't matter if he left it -- and punched in the number to the Boneyard.

Pops answered on the third ring. "You good?" No question Pops knew who the call was from. Each team had some kind of safeguard in place in case they needed something immediately.

"Fine. Need Cain."

"Sure thing. Hang on." There was blaring music in the background and raucous laughter. Then everything was muffled for a few seconds. He heard a door closing in the background, then Cain's voice came over the earpiece. Stunner put him on speaker phone.

"Stunner. Is Suzie OK?"

"Fine. I have someone here who thinks you need to hear him out."

"I see. Any idea what it's about?"

"Yeah. He's warning me off Suzie. Says his dad's got shit going on with Alex and his crew at Argent. Says he can get us discounted stuff and get ExFil in on some weapons testing if I abandon Suzie here."

"You gonna?"

"No. But figured you should be the one to tell the little fuck the way it is. Above my paygrade."

"You on a burner?"

"Yeah. Givin' him the phone so you can 'splain. I'm headed up to Suzie now."

"Take care of my girl, Stunner. You know we have your back if you need it."

Stunner snorted. "Don't need it with this punk. Though if you wanna send Willa, she could use the practice."

"Doubt Trucker would let me, but I'll give her the option. Now, who is this guy? More importantly, does he even know what Argent Tech is?"

"Name's Jake Salisberry, and I doubt it. If he did" -- Stunner met Jake's ever-widening eyes with his own piercing gaze --"he'd know that Argent makes the tech that goes into the weapons. Not the weapons themselves. But then, he *is* a stupid-ass motherfucker."

"I'm also guessing that he doesn't know Giovanni Romano is the one who practically forced Suzie into MIT in the first fuckin' place. You realize, if it hadn't been for him gettin' all pissy that she broke into their system when she was seventeen, she'd be at home right now? How'd he put it?"

"Just because she can break into a highly sophisticated, highly classified network doesn't mean she doesn't need to learn how to do it in a way she'll never get caught."

There was a silence before Cain said, "Hmm. Not sure he said it exactly like that, but I'm pretty sure that's how she took it."

"As evidenced by the fact that the next time she did it, it took him three days to figure out he'd even been hacked."

"OK, yeah. I remember now. Anyway. Put the dipshit on the phone. We'll see if his daddy's more connected than me."

"He might have you there, brother," Stunner said, a smile teasing his lips, but he managed to keep it tightly under wraps. "But I guarantee your contacts can take his contacts."

Stunner tossed the phone to Jake. "Have a nice chat with the man who won the protective father of the year award and just happens to have several full teams of lethal soldiers at his beck and call." Had he ever had such a long conversation with anyone? He sighed. He was getting soft. He'd wanted to intimidate the shithead. He'd succeeded, but had given away *tons* of information.

Wincing as he opened the stairwell, Stunner decided he'd fooled around long enough. It was time to get things settled with Suzie.

* * *

How long did it take to get his clothes from the car? Suzie knew she'd been a bitch. Run-ins with Jake or pretty much anyone else in her building always put her in a bad mood. Honestly, she had no idea what she'd done to get on literally everyone's bad side. It must be one of her talents.

There was a knock at the door, and she jumped. A quick look out of the peephole told her it was Stunner. No real surprise, but it wasn't until that moment she realized she'd half expected him to abandon her again. God, she was pathetic!

She opened the door and just resisted the urge to throw herself at him. Still, she let out a breath that made her lungs burn and her throat tighten.

Stunner shut the door and tossed his bag on the floor, pulling her into his arms the first second he could. He kissed the top of her head and squeezed her tightly. "Sorry. Didn't mean to take so long."

Was he trembling? No. She had to be wrong. It was her trembling, quaking in her shoes. Surprisingly, it wasn't from fear. Despite her past, despite doing everything in her power to suppress this side of her nature out of fear of where her mind would go. The second Stunner wrapped those wonderfully strong arms around her, her mind simply embraced the sensations even as she embraced the man.

She tilted her face up to him, accepting his kiss. His growl thrilled her even as the tenderness he showed her filled her with warmth and a love she'd only ever hoped existed. Funny. She'd always known Stunner loved her, but she felt like everything was brand new now. Like this was the first time he'd ever held her. In a way, she supposed it was. There was expectation in the air that had never been there at any other time.

Cupping her face in one hand, Stunner guided her, showing her what they both needed. He was patient, never rushing her, but she knew he wanted to. The dampness of his shirt over his sweat-slickened skin proved that.

"Need you naked, baby," he said, his voice that gruff, sexy growl she loved. He pulled back, cupping the other side of her face with his other hand so that he had complete control of her. His hands were so big, they nearly covered her whole head. "Do you trust me?"

She smiled, realizing she did. "Only you, Stunner. I trust only you with this."

He nodded gravely, never looking away from her eyes. "If you get scared, you say so. We'll stop and talk about what I did to frighten you. I'll never get angry, honey. Never."

"I know. Besides, I don't think it's possible for you to scare me. You've taken care of me through some of the worst times in my life. I think we can both manage this."

He nodded once, then scooped her up and headed to the bedroom. Suzie buried her face in his neck, inhaling the woodsy smell of him. The underlying hint of gasoline fumes were still present, even though he'd obviously taken great pains to hide that part of himself from the outside world, and it made her smile.

When he sat her on the bed she looked up at him, watching intently as he slid the buttons carefully from the little holes in his shirt. His fingers seemed too big, but were dexterous. She couldn't help but wonder how those fingers would feel on her body. What wicked things would he do to her? How much would she enjoy them?

Suzie had seen Stunner's naked torso several times. Usually when he was working out or they went swimming together. Now, every glorious inch of muscle-hardened, tattooed skin he revealed made her want to take a bite out of him. Her mouth actually watered, and she caught herself licking her lips. When he chuckled, she knew she'd been caught.

"Just as anxious to see you, Suz. You don't start strippin', might do it for you."

"Yes," she breathed. "Strip. All over that."

Again, he chuckled, but as she bared her body before him, all traces of humor vanished. His eyes got wide, then narrowed with intensity. He finished undressing in a rush, nearly tripping over his pants as he kicked them and his boxer briefs aside as he reached for her.

Suzie felt small next to his much larger frame. Stunner was all muscle and brawn. A dusting of hair roughened his skin and abraded hers as she slid beneath him. Automatically, Suzie's legs wrapped around Stunner's hips. His fingers threaded through her hair, and he lowered his mouth to hers once again.

This kiss was hungry, almost desperate. His tongue dipped into her mouth and lapped at her insides, stroking over and over and over again. Suzie had never willingly kissed another person until Stunner. She craved to be able to please him in everything, but especially kissing. Probably because she loved his kisses so much. He seemed to know every little thing she loved about it. He seemed to know when to lick, when to suck, when to nip her bottom lip sharply. Strangely, he always seemed to do it just before panic seized her. Always, the little hurt brought her back to the moment. To Stunner.

"Christ," he muttered. "So fuckin' sweet…"

He kissed her once more before trailing his lips down her jaw to her throat. Then lower. She lay on her back, her small breasts bare to his gaze and touch. He'd pressed their chests together with his weight, but now, he was headed there deliberately with his mouth. Suzie couldn't seem to catch her breath. She panted, little whimpers escaping. Right up until the moment his mouth closed over one nipple.

With a sharp gasp, Suzie's hands flew to Stunner's hair. She tried to tangle her fingers there, to hold him firmly to her, but with his hair cut in a high and tight military cut, she couldn't get the grip she wanted. She wanted to tell him he was letting his hair grow back out, but couldn't form the words. All she could do was moan and whimper as he worked magic with his teeth and tongue.

For his part, Stunner seemed to have devolved from the sleek, sophisticated get-up back to the caveman she knew he was at heart. She wanted the caveman. That was the Stunner she knew and loved beyond measure.

He moved from one breast to the other. Then back. Then again. It wasn't long before Suzie was panting, squirming, and screaming. Mindless with pleasure. Never in her wildest dreams did she ever think she'd be this lost in a man. Especially during sex. She did know that, if he stopped what he was doing, if he made her wait for this moment, she'd die. She'd never wanted anything more in her entire life.

Stunner continued to move down her body. His hands cupped both her breasts as he kissed her belly. Legs still spread, Suzie thrust her pelvis at him. It was a purely instinctual move on her part, but she knew that was where she wanted his attention. Stunner was as gentle as if he were touching a newborn, but his growls and snarls as he grew closer to her center let her know how eager he was for her.

* * *

Nothing in Stunner's life had ever been so important as giving Suzie this pleasure. He still thought it was way too soon, but he couldn't wait any longer. She knew he wouldn't hurt her. Knew he would always protect her no matter what happened between them now. If she got afraid or decided she didn't want this -- or him -- she knew she could. But Stunner had every intention of making her so mindless for him that she would never even contemplate his stopping.

She smelled heavenly. A combination of honeysuckle and roses that'd had him hard since the second he caught that scent. She always smelled like that. Oh. And fresh rain. God, the woman had driven him crazy for two fucking years! Being gentle with her was an absolute must, but his baser instincts were driving him hard to claim her. To fuck her hard and fast, then to come inside her and bury himself deep.

Her soft little cries were like that of a pleasured kitten. Her little nails digging into his shoulders were her claws.

The second he reached her sweet little pussy and draped her legs over her shoulders, she let out a sharp cry. Before he'd even touched her.

He looked up at her, needing to see her soft, golden-brown eyes. Hers were wild, large as saucers but filled with lust and need rather than fear.

"That's my girl," he praised. Stunner was surprised he was able to get out actual words. His ears roared with the need to be inside her. But, to deny himself a taste of the heaven her pussy promised it would be was simply not something he could do. "Need to taste you."

"Yes," she gasped. "Oh, God, yes! Please!"

Her pussy was bare, silky as her lovely thighs. Stunner ran his face over her mound several times, unable to help himself. He wanted to feel as much of her as he could. To savor the experience even though his instinct hammered at him to claim her. If this never happened again, he wanted to remember every fucking second of his intimate time with her. To him, Suzie was everything good in his life. She deserved as much pleasure and anticipation as he could give her.

"Smell so fuckin' good," he murmured. He tried to calm himself, but his voice came out more a growl than anything else. God! Could he do this? Without frightening her to death?

"Stunner," she whimpered. "Kiss me there." Her words were mostly a whisper. Like she could hardly make herself say the words. Likely she had to really work at it. Or, hopefully, she was so lost in the moment she just let go. Stunner decided to push her a little. He knew what women liked. He just had to feel her out and discover what she liked the most. He suspected dirty talk would be a real turn-on for her. At least, if done gently.

"You want me to lick your sweet little pussy?" He placed a kiss just above her clit, teasing her with what the kiss could have been. "Want my tongue licking between your lips? Just like when I kissed your mouth?"

"Yes! Oh, God, please Stunner! Please do that!"

"Tell me what you want, baby. Say the words."

"I -- you want --" Her eyes widened in shock. Still, there was a spark of interest there. "I can't say that!"

"You can, baby. Tell me what you want me to do." He did his best to calm his voice, so he sounded smooth. Like he'd practiced all the way here from Palm Beach. "I'll do whatever you want, as long as you tell me."

"I-I want you to…" She trailed off, swallowing. "I want you to lick my pussy."

God! Could she be sexier? With a groan of defeat, Stunner did exactly as she asked. He licked her from opening to clit. Then again. Suzie thrashed in his arms so that he had to clamp his forearms over her thighs to keep her still.

"Fuck, girl. So fuckin' good!"

Finally, he just set in to feast. He put his mouth over her whole pussy, sucking and lapping at the cream she gave him. It was like lighting a fire to the driest hay field imaginable. They were both engulfed in flames.

Suzie screamed, locking her ankles around Stunner's neck, her fingers buried in his short hair. Stunner snarled and growled, licking her pussy like it was his first meal after a long fast. His arms clamped tighter around her thighs, holding her open to him. She bucked against him, rubbing her clit over his lips. Her pussy gushed at him. Stunner knew she was close. He wanted her there, but didn't want her to fall over the edge. Not yet. Not until he was inside her.

He pulled back, much to Suzie's obvious dismay. She tried to hold him to her with her legs, but he ducked underneath. When she screeched at him -- something he'd delight in reminding her of later -- he batted her legs apart and wrapped her in his arms. Scooting them up the bed, he held her even tighter until he realized she might not be able to breathe.

"NO!" she gasped. "Hold me tighter!"

"Don't want to hurt you, Suz. Not ever."

"Then fuck me, Stunner. I'm hurting because you're not inside me."

How could he deny her?

Stunner had planned on taking his time. So far, he was able to pat himself on the back for a job fucking well done. But now, he was having trouble.

"I need to get a condom, Suz. You gotta let me go a second."

"No!" She was breathing hard, sweat beading on her delicate skin. She moved her tiny hands to his face, cupping him firmly. "Nothing between us, Stunner. Just me and you. We don't need anything else."

Fuck. Shit. *Goddamn*!

With a quick nod, Stunner let his cock find the entrance to her wet little cunt…

And he slid home.

They both cried out, but never broke eye contact. Suzie's gaze was focused intently on his. She didn't seem to be in any pain. There was no fear in her lovely eyes. For that, Stunner thanked every deity he'd ever heard about. The last thing he wanted was for her to go someplace dark and sinister. Someplace he wasn't.

"Still with me, Suz?"

"Always."

It was exactly what he needed. Stunner began to move inside her. His hips found a slow, sensual glide, moving inside her at an unhurried pace. How the fuck he managed it, Stunner knew would always be a fucking mystery. He was flying on blind instinct. The second he got inside her, his mind calmed somewhat. There was still this driving urgency to claim her, but his inner beast seemed to be satisfied just surrounded by all her wet heat.

Suzie had moved her hands back to his shoulders, digging her little nails into the muscles there. Stunner loved it. She was a demanding lover, not the tentative, scared little thing he was expecting. Thank God too, because he knew this slow and steady pace wasn't going to cut it much longer. For either of them.

Sure enough, once her body adjusted to him, Suzie wrapped her legs around him once again and locked them at the small of his back. Her heels dug into him, urging him on. He followed her, letting her set the pace. The faster and harder she urged him, the more he liked it. It wasn't long before he was riding her hard, giving them both a teeth-clattering ride.

"Stunner," she gasped. "I'm going to… gonna…"

"That's it, baby. Let it happen. Come for me."

"Unnnhh!" She groaned, reaching hard for her peak. Sensing she needed something more, Stunner rolled them, letting her sprawl over him. He still had his arms wrapped tightly around her, surging up into her hard. The new position seemed to be just what she needed. Three strokes later, Suzie screamed her climax.

Her body clamped down on his, milking him, commanding him to follow her. He did. With a brutal yell, Stunner let himself go, emptying his cum into her in spurt after spurt.

Both of them lay there, breathing heavily. Never had Stunner known such inner peace. His mind was silent of all the demons inside him, telling him he could never be good enough for any woman, let alone one so dear to him. For those precious moments, he was completely and utterly at peace with himself. Happy, even.

After several minutes, just before Stunner knew he was going to doze off, Suzie giggled. Her breathing had settled somewhat but she made no effort to move.

"I think I might have broken something." She didn't sound in pain, but Stunner loosened his hold on her.

"Did I hurt you, baby?" He noticed his voice was no longer that pleasing timbre he'd worked so hard to perfect. It was back to the gruff and growly one that was more natural to him.

"Goodness, no! That was the most wonderful thing I've ever experienced. I'm just not sure I can move now."

"No need for you to, baby. I'll take care of you."

"Yeah? Well, I'd love to say I'd take care of you, too, but I'm serious when I say I can't move. My body feels like jelly."

Stunner rolled gently. When she was on her back looking up at him, he brushed damp tendrils of hair off her forehead. "Don't worry. I'll get you cleaned up, then we'll rest for a while." She looked at him for a moment, a calculating look in her eyes. He stilled. "Uh, oh. I know that look."

She blinked, looking startled. "What look?"

"That look," he said. "You're about to get me into trouble. Aren't you?"

"You mean more trouble than you're already in?" She giggled. "Pretty sure your president would take exception to what we just did together." His president. Her dad.

Stunner winced, though he knew he had Cain's blessing to be with his daughter or he wouldn't have been there in the first place. "Don't remind me."

"I wasn't wanting to use super glue to make you a glitter beard. I was just wondering if you had your bike with you."

He raised an eyebrow. "Just so happens it's in a trailer parked in the driveway of the house I'm renting. What did you have in mind?"

She ran her palms over the smattering of hair across his chest. "I just thought you might take me on a ride. The nights here are cool but refreshing this time of year. Besides, I think I'd like to show Rebecca and Georgina I'm not a wuss."

Stunner went still. "They called you a wuss?"

"Well, in their defense, I kind of am. At least in some areas. I don't like scary men. They think that makes me weak."

He frowned. "I'm a scary man."

"You are not." She laughed. "You're Stunner. My very own badass biker."

With a sigh, he rolled off her, sitting beside her on the edge of the bed. "You know I'll do whatever you want, baby. But I'm telling you right now, if they call you names again, I won't be responsible for what happens next."

"Yeah," she said, sitting up. "Dad told me about the fight. He said you were pretty angry."

He snorted. "Not sure angry's the word I'd use."

"Homicidal?"

"Probably."

To his surprise, she grinned. "Can't say I'd be sorry. But I don't want you in trouble. Though if you did kill him, I'm sure Daddy would take care of it. He says killing isn't an easy thing, but sometimes it has to happen."

"Your dad's a smart man."

"I think so." She smiled brightly. "You gonna go get your bike or what?"

He grinned. "As you wish, Buttercup. Meet me outside in half an hour."

Chapter Five

On the way to the rent house, Stunner stopped by a local drug store. One thing he'd learned to always have around was a burner phone he could use with no notice if he had to keep off the grid. It was a simple model with only the basics. Call. Text. No GPS or Internet. The phone could still be pinged on a cell tower, but it was in no way linked with him. If he used it, all he had to do was make sure his regular cell was off. He usually removed the battery from his regular phone, if possible, as an added precaution.

Dialing the Boneyard number, he waited for Pops to pick up. He did so on the third ring. "Stunner," was all he said before hanging up. Pops would get the caller ID and pass it on to Data. With Bones notified, he also shot off a one-word text to a different number. *Raylan* went out to the current burner cell of El Diablo. He wanted to cut ties with the man completely, but just couldn't. Two things kept him from doing so. First, El Diablo didn't let anyone cut ties unless he killed them, and Stunner wasn't dead yet. Second, the man had helped Stunner when he was at the lowest point in his life. He couldn't simply break away completely.

Sure enough, a few seconds after sending off the text, a one-letter response came.

K

Raylan was a code. Any time Stunner had to give out his identity over El Diablo's phone, he changed the name he was using. His code names went by alphabet. It was simply R's turn, and Stunner loved the series "Justified," so that was the name he chose. Stunner didn't pretend to know how the other man kept up with it all, but he did.

With that done, he headed to his house to change clothes from the stuffy suit into jeans and a black T-shirt. His tats showed, but he figured Suzie wouldn't be too put off. He put the truck in the garage and rolled his bike from the trailer. The Fat Boy Harley was his favorite of anything he'd ever ridden.

Taking out the second helmet he'd brought with him on the off-chance Suzie wanted to ride with him, he grinned. Pink. She'd picked it out and decorated it herself. Pink. With a Bones MC rocker on the back. Everyone in Bones had shaken their head the first time she'd worn it, but no one had dared berate her for it. Not because they were afraid of Cain or him, but because Suzie was loved by every single member of the club. Now, given that he knew she was taking some heat from other students in her apartment, he thought about bringing one of the plain black ones in the storage cabinet. Normally, he'd have insisted on her wearing one not marked with Bones colors, but, with it being pink, any MC in the area wouldn't look at it twice. He pulled out a plain black leather vest for him, a leather jacket for her, stuffed it all in a saddle bag, and off he went.

Fuck it. If they gave her trouble, he'd dish out more to them. He was proud of her. Proud to be with her.

That done, he drove back to Suzie's building to wait. She still had ten minutes, and he didn't expect her right away. Her room was on the front side of the building so, if she was watching for him and was ready, she'd be on the way down.

The second he pulled up next to the building, two women from earlier, dressed to kill in slinky short dresses, sauntered out. Both of them had eyes on him. One was a skinny redhead. The other blonde woman had tits but no ass. Both had legs so long and skinny he had to wonder how they held up their own weight.

He held out hope that, maybe, they were headed to someone behind him until they parked themselves next to his bike. Apparently they hadn't learned their lesson. Stunner didn't dare look up. If Suzie saw, she'd be hurt. Then he'd have to hurt someone and, while he had no problem seeing a woman hurt if she deserved it, he had no desire to be the one to actually do the hurting. Oh, he talked a big game, but the worst he could bring himself to do under normal circumstances was to tell the bitches off. Hurting Suzie like these two could by being near him was a murdering offense.

"Hey there, big guy," the redhead said. "I'm Becca."

His head came up. "Rebecca?" When her smile became as wide as a Cheshire cat, he knew he was right. He turned to the blonde. "You must be Georgina."

"I am," she said silkily. "I know we've never *really* met because I'd never forget a man like you. No matter how drunk." They both giggled, draping themselves over each other. There was a time in Stunner's life when he'd have gone for that kind of thing. More than one woman at a time had been a nice pastime every once in a while, but not now. All he could think of now was how much trouble he'd be in if Suzie caught him fraternizing with the enemy.

"Heard 'bout you."

"Only naughty things, I hope," Rebecca said in a silky voice.

"No," Stunner said succinctly before looking back down at the control panel on his bike, fiddling with switches. When the pair didn't take the hint, he took out his phone and sent off a text to Suzie.

Need help. Bec and Grgna. Out front.

"No?" Rebecca asked, her eyes wide as if surprised. "Do tell."

He looked up at the pair, careful to keep his gaze cold and flat. "Heard you're smart. Have to be to get into grad school at MIT. Also heard you're more interested in partying than studying. Bit on the lazy side." He waited until that last sank in and Rebecca's face started to darken with anger. "Don't like lazy bitches. Never make for a good fuck. Expect me to do all the fuckin' work." He looked them both up and down, frowning. Then he shook his head. "No. Don't like lazy fucks."

That got both women sputtering in indignation. Thank goodness, too, because Suzie came be-bopping out of the building looking good enough to fucking eat. As he drank her in, Stunner actually licked his lips in anticipation.

She had on a flirty skirt that swished around her long, toned legs and hit her just above the knees. Her top was a white tank with thin straps, the material hugging her breasts to perfection. She skipped over to him, pushing her way past the two other women.

"Fuck, woman," he said as he dismounted. He reached for her, pulling her into his arms tightly and lifting her off the ground. "I'm gonna eat you up tonight. Right here on my fuckin' bike." Too late he realized he'd said that in front of the other women. While he could give two fucks, Suzie might be embarrassed. Thankfully, she just giggled.

"Promises, promises." She reached up and pulled him down for a brief kiss. "Did you bring my helmet?"

He grunted, reaching for the bright pink dome he'd lashed down to the back seat. "Jacket's in the bag. Bit cool for that top, but you will *not* change."

"You like?" She twirled around, the silky material floating out, giving a lovely glimpse of her creamy thighs. He could faintly see smudges where he'd gripped her too hard and barely stifled a wince.

"Very fuckin' much, baby. But... did I hurt you earlier?"

She blinked several times. "What? No! Why would you say that?"

"I saw a couple bruises on your inner thighs. You sure?"

Her smile was at once bright and sexy as fuck. A woman who'd gotten exactly what she wanted and was thoroughly satisfied. "Oh, absolutely. In fact, I hope to repeat the experience very, very soon."

"Wow," Rebecca said, sarcasm dripping from her voice. "Didn't know you were a such a slut, Suzie. I thought you were afraid of scary men?" She and Georgina giggled, nudging each other like they'd scored a point.

Suzie whipped her head to look at the pair. "Oh! I forgot you were here." She gave the pair a little wave. "Stunner's not scary." She looked at him and tilted his head. "Well, not always. And never with me." She leveled her gaze on the pair once more. This time, her gaze was as disapproving as her father's could be when he wanted to intimidate. "He's only scary to people who fuck with me."

Stunner took that as his cue to growl and bare his teeth. Childish, but effective. The two women swallowed and backed off a step.

Finally, Rebecca rallied. "Whatever. You two losers have fun fucking in the park. We'll make sure the police arrest you." She grabbed Georgina's arm. "Come on." She gave Stunner another once-over.

"Dumb bastard probably doesn't know how to use what little package he has anyway."

Georgina lingered, looking from Stunner to Suzie and back again. "No," she finally said, tugging her arm away from Rebecca. "I think he does. But I don't think any other woman but Suzie will ever find out." Instead of going with Rebecca, she nodded once at Suzie, muttered an apology of sorts, then went back inside the building.

"Sorry if I said something I shouldn't have," Stunner said softly. He'd managed to find that smooth, deep voice again. "Never wanted to embarrass you."

Suzie stood on her tiptoes and wrapped her arms around his neck, pressing her body tightly against him. There was nothing Stunner could do other than wrap his arms around her. "You didn't embarrass me. I'm proud to be your woman. And I fully expect you to make good on your promise to take me on your bike."

And just like that, his cock, which had been at half-mast already, was hard as iron. "Fuck, woman." He pressed her body harder into his, so there was no question whether or not he wanted her. "I'll be lucky to make it somewhere private before I lay you over the handlebars, push up your skirt, and devour your sweet pussy again." He rubbed her bottom through the skirt, then frowned. "Suzie…" He swallowed, then squeezed her ass. "Are you… are you wearing panties?"

She shrugged. "Didn't see any need for them. Figured you'd just take them off first chance you got."

He bent his head to give her a hard, lingering kiss. "You figured right."

With a grin, she snagged the jacket he had for her. "Come on. I want to ride with you. See if it makes me just a little bit horny."

"Fuck. Me." Stunner scrubbed a hand over his face. "I think I've created a monster."

They rode until dark. At least three hours. Just taking I-95 to I-93 around Cambridge and into Boston. They went through the Blue Hills Reservation in the south, up past Burlington in the north. Then they cut down through Middlesex Fells Reservation back to Boston. Over and over again. More than once, Suzie slid her hand over his crotch, stroking his cock through his jeans. She giggled and laughed throughout the entire ride. Stunner was struck at how complete he felt. He'd known she was his before, but this sealed the deal. Suzie was everything he'd ever wanted in a woman. He might not be the man she deserved, but he would do his best to make himself into that man. Whatever it took to get there, he'd do it.

* * *

Had she thought college sucked? Well, technically, it still did. But with Stunner back with her, Suzie had a new perspective on things. She wasn't afraid anymore. She wasn't lonely.

They'd ridden for hours, and she'd loved every single second of it. When he pulled into the garage of the house he said he was renting, she grew eager to get inside. She knew once there, he'd take her to his bed and they wouldn't leave it until she had to go to work. Which would be Monday morning. That gave her a couple of days to simply enjoy Stunner and her new relationship with him. Which was to say sex. She wanted to spend the entire weekend having more of that glorious sex he'd shown her earlier.

The second the garage door was down she hopped off the bike and took off her helmet. With a grin, she shrugged out of her jacket and hung it up next to Stunner's own. Instead of getting off the bike, however, Stunner scooted back slightly and crooked a finger at her.

"What?" She grinned as she asked the question.

"Get over here." His voice had gone back to that husky rumble she loved.

"Why? I thought we'd go in and have some more fun."

"Not yet." He reached out and snagged her arm, dragging her over to him. He lifted, her, guiding her to put one leg over the seat and straddle him, sitting backwards on the bike. "Told you I was gonna eat you out on my bike. Raise the skirt."

"Oh…" This surprised her even as it aroused her. She hadn't really thought he'd do this. In their world, the bike was sacred. And he wanted to make love to her on it?

She pulled her skirt up. With a growl, Stunner cupped her bare ass in his hands and lifted her to him. Her shoulders rested over the handlebars, her skirt was now around her waist, and Stunner's mouth descended to her pussy and he sucked.

Suzie gasped, her hands going to his thighs to anchor herself. He sucked and licked at her clit, occasionally dipping into her opening to lap her up. Her feet found his thighs as well, and she was able to support herself while he did his thing.

"Gonna come for me. Come hard, baby."

"Stunner!" She thrashed her head, wanting to hold off because she didn't want it to be over. But he was merciless, sucking her lips, nibbling her clit. He thrust two fingers inside her, hitting a spot that set her off like a bottle rocket. Her screams echoed around them, her body tensing and bucking against him.

"Fuck! *Fuck*!" He continued to eat her pussy, but he moved beneath her. She heard the zip of his jeans as he shifted. Then he knocked her legs off his thighs and positioned her so that, with one solid thrust, he was inside her. "Here," he said, pulling her up. Her legs dangled over his, not touching anything. He quickly urged them around his waist. "Keep them there. Don't want you burnin' yourself on a fuckin' pipe."

It took him a few seconds to get them both where he wanted, but the second he did, he urged her to ride him. It was difficult, but he stretched her *so good*! With each movement, her pleasure built. The longer they went, the more Stunner growled. The faster he moved. He shoved up her tank, exposing her breasts to his big hands. He kneaded and squeezed until he finally just wrapped his arms around her body and brought his mouth to one puckered nipple.

That was all it took. A second rush of pleasure overtook her, crashing in wave after wave of tremendous sensation. She gasped in a breath, trying desperately to scream but couldn't. When she finally did, the sound exploded from her lungs. Which apparently triggered Stunner's own bellow of completion. He came inside her, his cum filling her hotly. He pulled her as close to him as he could, his cock still pulsing out seed.

"Goddamn! Fuck!" His shouts were forceful, but shaky. As if she'd been the one to drain him of his powerful strength. The fact was, she felt like she was about the consistency of Jell-O at the moment.

They both gasped, trying to catch their breath. She smiled up at him. There was no way to hide the stars in her eyes. Stunner was magnificent. Everything he did, Suzie knew he did for her in some way. His haircut, shaving his beard, the clothes… all of it. He'd done that for her. He'd pleasured her because he knew she enjoyed it. Not to say he didn't enjoy himself as well, but she knew that, had she not shown some sign that she'd loved what they'd done earlier, this encounter on his bike would never have happened. He was showing her how wondrous and exciting sex with the right man could be. He knew her past and was careful of her, but he also wanted her to experience life.

Hadn't he told her that in the past? When she was afraid of something, of the men in Bones or even going off to college, Stunner had always encouraged her and reinforced that her family would always be there for her. He'd be there for her. He never put her in a compromising or dangerous position, and he never pushed her beyond what she could handle. He'd taught her by his actions that she could do much more than she thought. She was a strong woman. She just had stronger backup.

They were brought out of their reverie by a tentative knock at the garage door. "Uh, Mr. Stunner? Everything all right in there?" Stunner groaned. The elderly next-door neighbor was the owner of the property. Last thing he wanted to do was alarm the old guy or to disrespect him in any way. He was pretty sure he'd done both.

Suzie giggled, giving him a soft kiss before climbing off the bike and righting her skirt. "Do I have cum trickling down my legs?" The question was asked with a cheeky grin. Stunner sighed and shook his head.

She went to the door and opened it, leaving the bay door closed. "Hi," she said. "I'm so sorry we disturbed you." She stuck her hand out to the older man. "My name's Suzie Gill."

"Tucker Hargis," he said. "The wife and I heard someone scream and thought…"

Suzie's hands went to her cheeks, embarrassed, though Stunner thought it was more for effect than anything else. He quickly checked to make sure he hadn't forgotten to zip his fly and climbed off his bike. If she was going to face the elderly man, he could too, Goddammit. "Ohmigod! I'm so sorry! We were… uh… well, Stunner is my fiancé, and we haven't seen each other in a while, with me being at school, and…" She trailed off, looking over her shoulder as Stunner came to stand behind her, putting his hand gently on her arm.

"I apologize, Mr. Hargis. We meant no disrespect."

Mr. Hargis just waved his hand in the air, dismissing the perceived infraction. "No need to apologize, Stunner." He winked at Suzie. "She's a looker. Any man who could wait to be kissin' on such a beautiful girl don't want her bad enough. I was just afraid someone was hurt." He grinned. "I'll remember if I hear the same noises comin' from the house."

"Much appreciated, sir," Stunner said, hugging Suzie close. "She's my woman."

"Can't say I'm glad of that," Mr. Hargis said, scratching his head through the sparse white hair. "If she wasn't, I'd try to take her home with me." He grinned, addressing Suzie. "He don't treat you right, honey, you come find me. I can't take him. Too old. But I'll spoil you like you deserve."

"You tryin' to take my woman, old man?" Stunner tried to keep the grin from tugging at his lips.

"Nope. But I ain't sayin' I won't try in the future."

There was no help for it -- Stunner not only smiled, he chuckled. "I'd tell you to get out, but it's your property. Pretty sure you should be the one tellin' me to leave."

"Ain't doin' that, son. So long as you're good to your girl there."

"No worries there, Mr. Hargis."

Once the man was gone, Suzie burst into giggles. "I think he meant it, Stunner. He'll take me home and spoil me." She shook a finger at him. "You better indulge me in as much sex as I want, or I know just who to tell."

He scooped her up. "I got that covered, darlin'." She squealed when he buried his face in her neck and blew a raspberry. God, he loved her!

Once inside, Suzie kissed him once more, but pushed him firmly away when he would have started in again.

"I thought..."

"Don't misunderstand, Stunner. You thought right. But we have some things to address first." She led him to the couch and sat, tugging him down beside her. "Now. Tell me why you went to Florida without me."

Fuck. He'd hoped to avoid this. Not because he didn't want to give her the strict truth, but because he knew the truth would lead to other questions he *didn't* want to answer.

"Don't give me that look, Stunner. I deserve to know why you left without saying anything. More importantly, I deserve to know why you cut me off from you."

OK, *that* got to him. When she wanted to know why he'd not answered her properly, he knew how badly he'd hurt her. Those big, golden-brown eyes of hers glinted with unshed tears, and she looked up at him with a childlike look of hurt on her face. In that instant, he was back to the first time he'd ever seen her. Beaten and broken, Cliff and Daniel trying their best to protect her. He'd done his best by her then, making it possible for the boys to get all three of them out of Kiss of Death and to safety. She'd been a frightened little girl then. Now she was a grown woman, but the look of hurt was the same. She couldn't understand why she was being hurt then. She couldn't understand why Stunner had hurt her now.

"Baby, the truth is, you need a man better'n me. You were grown. Off to school. I was the one clinging to you, and you needed to live your life. Like your mama said. Giovanni did a good thing, makin' you apply to MIT." He sighed, scrubbing his hand over his face, still having trouble with the lack of a beard. "You don't need a scruffy, hardass biker in your life. You need someone like Giovanni or Azriel. That's the world you belong in." He shrugged. "That ain't me, darlin'."

She frowned, then tossed a pillow at him. "Asshole," she muttered. "You really think I'm that superficial?"

"I -- what?"

"Stunner, I don't want someone like the guys here. Sure, there are some who don't fit the mold, and I appreciate that. But I want *you*, Stunner. Not anyone in Shadow Demons, or at MIT. You. I just want you."

He pulled her into his arms, nuzzling her hair and neck. "You have me, baby. As long as you want me, you have me."

Chapter Six

The next two weeks were the happiest of Suzie's life. She taught her classes, put in her time with her students, and spent every single night with Stunner. The past two Friday nights, he'd insisted on dressing up and taking her to fine-dining establishments in both Cambridge and Boston. He'd dressed the part proudly, throwing his chest out when she tucked her hand into the bend of his elbow. Though he hadn't seemed to enjoy the food, he'd insisted on her trying every single thing on the menu that interested her. Everything she'd left, he'd packed up, and they'd taken it to local homeless shelters. It had to have cost a small fortune, but he'd done it twice with plans on doing it again when the weekend rolled around.

The second she finished her tutoring in the lobby Friday afternoon, she bounded up the stairs and burst into her dorm excitedly. They stayed at her place on Fridays because of her tutoring. It made it easier on her to finish up anything for the weekend and still have time to shower and change comfortably.

One look at Stunner's face, and she knew something was wrong. "Stunner?"

"I can't take you out tonight, baby. In fact, we should go back to my place where I know that little punk, Jake, can't get to you easily. I've got better security because I can surround the place with cameras."

"Jake? What's happened?"

He scrubbed a hand over his face. A gesture he was doing way too much lately. Until he started giving a damn about what Suzie's colleagues thought of him, he'd never given a damn about his behavior. Now, it was embarrassing. "I may have gone too far with Jake a couple of weeks ago, Suz."

"Did you hurt him? I mean, I haven't seen him in a while other than in passing, thank God, but you didn't kill him, and he's not in the hospital. Right?"

Deciding to push just a little, to find out where her limits were, he asked, "How much would it matter if I did?"

She raised her eyebrows. "To me? Not at all. But I don't want you in jail. I hear they have some rough people there." She grinned.

"Brat," he muttered. "Well, no. I didn't touch him physically. I might have implied otherwise if he so much as looked in your general direction, but I didn't actually touch him."

"So? I don't get it."

"So, Jake told his daddy he'd been threatened. His daddy is Markus Salisberry. Apparently he's a big deal… doing something. Don't know. Don't care. Anyway, Markus has a hard-on for Argent Tech. He's currently trying to stage a hostile takeover of Argent using Alex, Azriel, and Giovanni's association with ExFil and, more importantly, Cain as Bones' president as proof they cater to unsavory characters. Mainly because, apparently, one of Giovanni's protégés -- that would be you -- hired an ExFil operative -- me -- to intimidate Jake into leaving MIT. He also accuses me of 'mistreating' his son physically. Apparently, Jake has the bruises to prove it."

"That snake! I'll show the little fucker mistreatment!" She turned to go, but Stunner caught her.

"Just hang on, Suz."

"I'm not letting him get away with this! Can't Giovanni fight him?"

"Calm down, honey. You know Giovanni has everything under control. No one's taking Argent Tech away from those three. Markus Salisberry wants to play hardball, he just bit off more than he can chew with the Shadow Demons. Might have helped if he actually knew they were the Shadow Demons, but still."

That made her chuckle. Then she sobered. "So, what do we do?"

"About that? Nothing. But there's more. Apparently, I'm being watched. Giovanni and Data are working on it, but somebody's watching me. They're very well hidden and old school, staying off the tech. But occasionally whoever it is slips up. Gives an electronic report of some kind, and they leave a footprint. Data and Giovanni are on it, so I have no doubt they'll figure it out, but until then we need to get back to Kentucky. I want the best defensible place there is to keep you safe."

"I'll do whatever you want me to. You know I'm not going to fight you on that."

He gave a sharp nod. "Tomorrow we can head back. Data and Giovanni are on this. They'll figure out what we need to do next." He pulled her into his arms. "I'm sorry 'bout this, baby."

"Not your fault. But if I see Jake on the way out, I'm gonna kick him in the balls."

* * *

Stunner woke to the vibration of his phone on the nightstand. As usual, he was instantly awake. Suzie lay sprawled over him, clutching his chest, her leg draped over his thigh. Thankfully, she still slept.

He picked up the phone. "Yeah," he said.

"You need to get back to Kentucky. Right fuckin' now." That was Cain. He sounded equal parts pissed and worried. Hell, he sounded almost scared. "I've got

Bohannon, Sword, Viper, and Trucker on the way. Be ready to leave the second they get there."

"How long?"

"That's the fuckin' problem. Gonna take them at least thirteen hours to get there. That's hard ridin' and leavin' Trucker behind with the cage. You may not have that long."

"Explain."

"Someone's put a fuckin' hit on your fuckin' ass and a soft hit on Suzie. Kind of a take-her-if-you-see-her kind of thing."

Everything in Stunner went still. He clutched Suzie closer to him. He'd come so fucking close to complete happiness. Now this. Was his past finally catching up to him? If so, why did it include her? Sure, they could be trying to make him suffer, but if that had been the case, wouldn't it have been the other way around? Or at least a terminate order on both of them?

"You know who?"

"No. But Data and Zora are working with Giovanni. They'll figure it out, of that I have no doubt. Once we do, we'll hit the son of a bitch first, then take out his assassin."

"I've got a big-ass truck. I can load her up and head out in thirty. We'll meet the boys on the road."

"That'll probably be best. You alert enough to do this on your own?"

"Had a couple hours' sleep already. I can make it until we meet the boys. It will cut down the time we have without an escort in half."

"Good, then. Let me know the second you're on the road. You've got thirty."

He packed Suzie's laptop and a change of clothing before waking her gently. She murmured sleepily, but wrapped her arms around his neck without protest when he lifted her. Thank God the garage was attached to the house so he didn't have to take her out into the open. Even though it went against what he'd normally do, Stunner put her in the back seat, asleep on her side, and tucked her in with a quilt. He kissed her temple before shutting the door and climbing into the driver's seat.

The truck he'd brought was a black Ford F-350 dual cab. The extra room should be comfortable enough she would sleep for a few hours. Thank goodness, too, because Stunner had to think.

The question was, who had done this? He could guess the why. But he honestly couldn't imagine who because he'd never left anyone alive who would come after him or El Diablo. That had been part of his job.

As he headed down the interstate, he cursed himself all kinds of a fool. He'd known something like this would happen. It didn't matter that he'd taken all the precautions he could, killed everyone he'd had to, he still had no right to put Suzie in this situation. He glanced back at her sleeping form. She looked like an angel laying there. So beautiful. Innocent of the things he'd done in life. She'd never hurt anyone. And she'd been hurt far too much early in life.

Stunner made a vow then. No matter what, he'd eliminate the threat to her, come clean with her father, and take whatever punishment he had to before he left. Then he'd make sure she was never in this kind of danger ever again.

Then he had a thought.

No. No, that couldn't be right.

Taking out his burner, he called El Diablo himself. The bastard answered on the first ring.

"Wondered when you'd call to tell me to back off."

"So, did you put out the hit in Salisberry's name or take it for him?"

"Neither. But I've been watching."

"Well, don't. I need you to back off."

Stunner could almost see the other man's grin. "Now, why would I do that? Someone has to keep an eye on you. You tend to get into trouble without it."

"Now ain't the time, motherfucker. Just back the fuck off!"

There was a silence before El Diablo spoke. "You haven't come clean, have you." It wasn't a question. When Stunner didn't respond, El Diablo continued. "You can always come home. Bring your woman with you. She'll be welcomed as well."

"I've never asked you for anything. But I'm askin' you now. Back. Off."

Before El Diablo could reply, or Suzie could wake up, Stunner snapped his phone shut. No sense tossing it out the window. It was obvious Stunner was headed back to Somerset and the Bones clubhouse. Hell, with El Diablo keeping tabs on him, the bastard probably knew the club was meeting Stunner to escort him and Suzie home.

There was so much rage and frustration pent up inside Stunner, he wanted to yell and pound the steering wheel. Fuck. He wanted to get out and find someone to take out his anger on. Hell, a tree would do. But he couldn't. He had to put distance between Suzie and Cambridge. And he had to bring them both closer to his brothers. Once they found out about Stunner, they might choose not to help him, but they'd never turn their back on Suzie. She needed their protection more than he did. He could take care of himself. Thank goodness, too, because it looked like he was going to be on his own.

* * *

Suzie had never slept so soundly. She had no memory of Stunner putting her in the truck or of them leaving the house. But she found herself three hours out of Cambridge by the time she woke.

She climbed over the center console and into the passenger's seat. As she snapped her seatbelt she glanced at Stunner. He'd been unfailingly kind, but he'd closed himself off like he used to. It was funny that she thought of it like that. "Like he used to" meant before the last two weeks. She'd gotten used to him sharing everything on his mind. She loved it.

Now, he was still affectionate -- he'd hardly let go of her hand since she'd settled herself -- but he hadn't offered information. She'd refrained from asking because she trusted him to let her know what she needed to know.

He stopped when he realized she was awake, but only long enough for her to pee beside the road. She protested loudly, but he calmly told her they couldn't risk stopping anywhere there were cameras. Naturally, she'd demanded to know why, but he'd just said he'd explain later. She'd huffed and muttered but had done her business and climbed back in the truck, and they were off again.

Once on the way, he'd explained that they were in danger but didn't know all the particulars. She got the feeling that was the strict truth, but that there were layers he was omitting. Still, she trusted him to do what needed to be done to protect them both.

To pass the time, she'd taken out her laptop to get some work done. Thanks to the little Internet hotspot Data had put together for her, she had decent Internet access. She worked for about two hours before a message popped up on her screen.

D Bonez: Stay on the DL. Stand by.

Data. Telling her to keep quiet and stand by? What the hell? She almost said something to Stunner, but he didn't look like he could take any more. He still reached over occasionally to rub her knee or put his hand around the back of her neck to knead her muscles gently, but he really looked like he was at a breaking point. A few minutes later Data contacted her again.

D Bonez: Sending encryption to your hotspot. Log on and follow the breadcrumbs.

She acknowledged and did as he told her. The message she retrieved chilled her to the bone. Someone was stalking Stunner. Not her. Whatever it was, was personal. And highly sophisticated. Together, Data and his wife, Zora, had managed to find some information but not enough to lead to a source. By them bringing Suzie in on the work, she knew they'd reached the end of anything they could do. She knew from experience that they'd likely used Giovanni, too. They were concerned and, really, anybody this intent on keeping hidden wasn't up to anything good. By giving this to Suzie, they acknowledged that they knew she'd keep digging until she figured it out. No matter what.

So she started digging through the dark web. Double checking the work already done and using it to form her own leads.

A few hours later, they met up with Bohannon, Sword, Viper, and Trucker. Or rather, it was more like she and Stunner never stopped and the other four turned around on the interstate and caught up to them. And that was it. Until that mad dash from Cambridge to Somerset, Suzie had never understood the term "hard driving." Hard driving was basically going as fast as they dared without getting noticed by the cops, and not stopping the entire trip. Even gas for the truck and bikes had been hauled with them in gas cans Trucker had in the bed of his truck.

And still she worked.

Through it all, Suzie did as she was told and clung as tightly as she dared to Stunner when she could while she worked. Every time she reached for him, she knew she clasped him tighter and tighter. She had the feeling he was slipping away from her, and she had no idea why.

"You good, baby?" The question caught her off guard. He hadn't spoken much during the entire trip, but he clung to her hand as hard as she did to him.

"Not really. What's happening, Stunner?" They were about fifteen minutes from the clubhouse and safety, and she was no closer to finding who was watching Stunner than she had been ten or so hours earlier. This was a conversation they should have had hours ago, but she'd wanted to give him every opportunity to do this on his own. Before they had to face the others, however, she had to get this out.

"I told you all I know."

"I've known you a long time. That's the first time you've ever truly lied to me." It hurt, and she didn't hide it from him. She thought she understood, but it didn't make it any less painful.

He didn't wince. The old Stunner she'd always known was back. Closed off as ever.

"We're almost home. You'll be safe there."

"I'm safe with you, Stunner," she said, backing up and trying again from a different angel. "No one, not even my dad, could protect me better than you. We're a team. Right?"

"Yes," was all he said.

"You've got to meet me halfway. I can take anything you tell me, but you've got to tell me all of it. Now. Before we have to face my father."

"I've got this. That's all you need to know."

Desperate, she decided to take the plunge. "Data gave me access to something he, Zora, and Giovanni have been working on. Did you know you have a stalker? Whoever they are, they're watching every single move you make." His gaze jumped to hers, but he said nothing, just slid his focus back to the road. But that muscle in his jaw ticked like crazy, and his eyes got a wild look to them. Yeah. He knew he was being hunted. And he did *not* want her to know who it was. "You know who it is. Don't you?"

"No."

"You're lying again." She was going to cry. She was losing him. And it worse than sucked.

"Suz, just let it go. Please. For me."

"Someone put a hit on you, and you're being stalked! I can't let this go! If they find you. If they…" She swallowed. "If they kill you…"

"They won't. And it's not the same person stalking me that put the hit on me. Just… just trust me on this. Please, baby."

She gave him what she knew was a desperate, panicked smile. "I can't risk it, Stunner. Please, just tell me and we'll fix it. Whatever it is. We'll fix it *together*."

Just her luck. He pulled onto the driveway leading to the clubhouse and fucking floored it. He was going to shut off this conversation any way he could. Since she wouldn't stop, he was forcing the issue.

They skidded to a stop, and Stunner shoved the door open. He stalked around to her side and helped her out. "Listen to me, Suzie." He glanced around, noting where everyone was. The whole of Bones were on alert, but gave Stunner and Suzie the seconds they needed. "This is all part of my past. All of it. Well, not the assassin part. That's all the Salisberrys. But this person watching me. It's all in the past. I swear, it won't touch you, but you've got to just let it go."

She shook her head. "If you're in danger from someone and I can stop it, you know I'm going to."

"I'm *begging* you, Suz. Let. This. Go."

Instead of waiting for an agreement, he pulled her into his arms and hugged her fiercely. She could have been imagining things, but she thought she felt his body trembling. Could have been her own, though. Because tears leaked from her eyes, and she was silently sobbing. He held her a few more moments, then turned, pulling her with him by the hand, and headed inside the clubhouse.

After leaving Suzie in Somerset, Stunner spoke with Cain for a few minutes, then got in the truck and left. Alone. No goodbyes, and he hadn't texted her. Which left her right back where they fucking started. If she hadn't been so worried and frustrated, she'd have cried her heart out. Instead, she turned her anger and fear into finding Stunner's shadow. Which meant she basically locked herself in her bedroom for the next two days.

She was just about to crash when she got the mother of all leads. Intellectually, she knew it was too easy. But she followed it like a bat out of hell. As fast as her fingers could fly across the keyboard, she tailed the son of a bitch. Later, she'd realize he'd let her find him, but in her sleep-deprived mind she'd spent the better part of three days hunting, and all that work had finally paid off.

When she finally put a name to the faceless stalker, it sent chills through her body and dread in her heart.

El Diablo…

Chapter Seven

The second Stunner pulled into the Bones compound, he knew he was caught. The place was locked down tight. They let him in, but no one welcomed him or even talked to him. Not even Shadow. The only thing anyone told him was that Cain wanted to see him. Great. After more than forty-eight hours on the road with no sleep, the last thing he needed was the confrontation he knew was coming. The thing he hated most about it was that Suzie had been the one to find him out. Or, at least, she'd been the one to find the path the others needed to find him out.

He'd gone back to Cambridge to get their things, including his bike. He'd cleaned everything out and stowed it in the trailer. Hauling that much on the frantic dash home would have used gas and sacrificed speed they couldn't afford. Now, he was bone tired. Weary in body, heart, and soul.

The second he stepped through the door, several Bones members behind him to guard against a retreat, he scanned the room for Suzie. The second their gazes collided she gave a cry and ran to him. Bohannon intercepted her, pulling her into his arms and whispering something in her ear. She shook her head, her gaze never leaving Stunner's. Bohannon gripped her chin and said something to her Stunner couldn't make out. He wasn't harsh with her, but he was firm, obviously impressing the importance of her following his instruction. Before she could defy him, Angel reached her, pulling the young woman into her arms, pulling her away from Stunner.

Never in his life had he felt more defeated. Not when he'd killed for the first time. Not when he'd left for Argentina at thirteen. Always, no matter what life threw at him, Stunner had put his shoulders back and pressed on. No retreat. No surrender. Now, he felt like he was crumbling under the weight of guilt and shame and loss. And it was his own damn fault.

"Come on, honey," Angel said. "This is club business. We need to leave."

"No! Mom, I'm not leaving."

"Baby, we have to."

"I said *no*! I'm not leaving Stunner. If this has to do with him, it has to do with me. We're a team." She turned to fix her gaze on Stunner's. He could see her lower lip trembling, like she knew something bad was coming, but refused to let him face it alone. Even if her parents wouldn't let her be at his side, she was standing solidly with him. That gave him hope when nothing else could.

"Enough," Cain said. His voice was soft but no less menacing. He shifted his body between Stunner and Suzie, but she moved to the side, not letting her father come directly between them. "You have anything you want to say to me, boy?"

"Would it matter now?" Stunner wasn't stupid enough to think that if he came clean now everything would go back to the way it was. One family had been lost to him forever two decades earlier. Now, he'd lost a second.

"No." There was no hesitation on Cain's part. "But you will tell me the extent of your dealings with El Diablo and exactly how much of Bones and ExFil has been compromised."

"Short version is --"

"Stop!" Cain held up a hand. "You don't get to give me the short version, Stunner. Start at the beginning and give me everything."

Stunner nodded, holding on to his composure as tightly as he could. "Before I do, will you tell me if the threat to Argent Tech has been contained?"

"It has. Salisberry had no clue who he was dealing with. Alex shut him down. Suffice it to say that, whatever Giovanni dug up on the man was enough to get him blackballed from every business he's ever been involved with. If he's not broke yet, he will be by tomorrow. Didn't negate the hit on you, but stopped any thought of a takeover of Argent. Now stop fuckin' stallin'."

"When I was thirteen, I watched my father kill my brother and my mother." Stunner heard Suzie take in a sharp breath, but her mother held her back when she tried to go to him. He glanced in her direction but then returned his gaze firmly to Cain's. "The details are a little fuzzy, but the bottom line is I killed him before he could kill me. We lived in an extremely secluded area of Oklahoma on a farm with over ten thousand acres, much of it woodlands. Again, the details aren't important, but I got rid of the body and scattered anything that remained in places where I knew the wildlife would take care of it. Anything I couldn't depend on the animals for, I burned." Stunner focused wholly on Cain, needing to see the man's reaction. And this wasn't the worst part by any means. So far, Cain held steady.

"Anyway, after it was done, I knew I couldn't stay in Oklahoma. The chances someone would find something were just too great. At thirteen, I couldn't imagine anything being worse than going to prison. So I fled to Argentina."

"Helluva place to pick. Why?"

He shrugged. "Foolishness. I read in school how, after World War II, there were Nazis who fled there and lived long and happy lives. I guess I figured if they could harbor that kind of murderer, no one would bat an eyelash at me."

"Christ," Cain swore, but nodded for Stunner to continue.

"Anyway, I lived there a year before I got into real trouble. Crossed the wrong gang. That's when I first made contact with El Diablo." When Cain said nothing, Stunner continued. "He could have killed me. Was supposed to kill me, but he didn't. Instead, he gave me a reprieve with the understanding that I work for him. I'd be loyal to only him for the rest of my life, do what he said, learn everything he had to teach me. In exchange for my service, he'd let me live. I found out later that the average life expectancy of people in his employ was about twenty. Since I'd started at fourteen, I wasn't expected to make it to sixteen. I was twenty-two before I realized I'd survived past what was technically the original agreement, not that I was stupid enough to mention it."

"What happened then?"

Stunner shook his head. "Not really sure. El Diablo gathered me and a man called the Reaper, El Segador, in for a meeting. Only the meeting was actually a ride back to the U.S. via private jet incoming to a private airstrip. There had been a falling out with him and whatever organization he worked for years earlier. It was why he was in Argentina. Once he had an excuse to get back to the States, he took it, moving me and Reaper with him.

"His plan was to start his own operation. To do that, he needed cover. While he was well dressed, well mannered, and well spoken, he didn't have the time to integrate into that kind of society. Instead, he figured he'd be better suited to some kind of gang. The decision to fit into an MC was an accident."

Stunner glanced around the room. It was hard to tell if they believed him or not, but no one was getting impatient or frustrated. That alone gave him the courage to continue.

"I was in Nashville. We were researching places and available resources. I'd been looking for some action out of sheer frustration and found myself in a biker bar. That's where I met Gremlin."

Suzie gasped and she sank into a nearby chair. Angel knelt beside her, urging her to leave, but she just shook her head. Her lovely face had gone pale, and her breathing was ragged. Stunner hated causing her pain, but it was best to just get it all out.

"The man had been beaten horribly. He was upright, but I had no idea how. The bruises on his face looked to be a couple days old, but it was hard to say. I had the feeling this guy was El Diablo's way in. The answer to setting up whatever operation he wanted. So I got him drunk and, as I'd hoped, he started talking.

"Kiss of Death was into all kinds of shady business dealings. But that wasn't important. The club was connected, ripe for the taking. That's what I needed information about. Apparently, there was an element inside the club not happy with the way the president, Crow, was running things. Gremlin thought they were all pussies, but then, Crow was his daddy.

"After that, he didn't give me anything else I wanted to hear. It was all rhetoric and nonsense. I was about to leave when he told me his daddy was the one who'd beaten him up. Naturally, given my past, that got my attention." He took a breath, glanced at Angel, then plunged on. "Apparently, Angel had just escaped. But he was hoping his dad would forgive him after the prize he'd just scored." Stunner found Suzie's gaze and locked on to her. "An innocent little eleven-year-old. The boys were an added bonus, but he was most excited about the girl. The plan was to mold her into the perfect club whore."

A tear dropped from Suzie's eye. Then one from the other eye. Her whole body shuddered. Angel had her arms wrapped around her daughter but was no longer trying to get the younger woman to leave the room.

"I got inside that very night. I found where the children were being held but managed to keep out of their sight. Assuming I was able to help them, I didn't want anyone identifying me with them so my cover would be intact. Any time Gremlin tried to get me to help with them, I found something else to do. I kept some of the men off them, but couldn't keep everyone safe. Not and set the club up for a takeover. I'd never done anything like that before, and I was in way over my head. I knew I needed help but getting in touch with either Reaper or El Diablo was tricky. I managed, though. After working out all the angles, we were convinced the only way to stop the whole fuckin' mess was to take them all down. Only, I had myself, Reaper, and El Diablo. Not nearly enough manpower.

"I knew there was no way any of the kids would last long enough for us to take over Kiss of Death. In fact, by that time, El Diablo had things in place for him to take over Black Reign. He just had to sit back and wait for things to move in his direction.

"So, I gave Cliff and Daniel the information they needed to get themselves and Suzie out of Nashville. I sent them to Bones because Bones had been one of El Diablo's targets of clubs to take over. He loved the idea of Bones being closely affiliated with ExFil. In his mind, that gave him far greater access to goods and muscle than any other club in the country if he could take it over. While Kiss of Death or Black Reign were the easier targets, Bones was the one he wanted most."

"Motherfuckin' Goddamn!" Cain swore, knocking a chair to the floor. Suzie whimpered, wrapping her knees to her chest and rocking herself. "How fuckin' compromised are we, you son of a bitch?" Stunner had never heard Cain so angry.

"You're not. I came to Bones to make sure the kids were OK. I got Shadow to vouch for me so you'd let me in to prospect, and I was able to keep an eye on all three of them."

"How did you know Shadow?"

"We grew up together in Oklahoma," Shadow supplied. "I had no idea he was even still alive. He seemed broken when he came here, and I wanted him to have a second chance, Cain. He was always a good person. Even now, I can't help but believe he had good intentions. Especially with Suzie."

"Fuckin' finish, Stunner. I want this over before we leave here tonight."

"Not much else to say. I made a home here. Fell in love with Suzie pretty soon after I got here, though not romantically or sexually. That came later. I always kept in touch with El Diablo, but only enough to fulfill my end of our bargain. I always gave non-answers. It's why I learned not to say much."

"Go on."

"After Magenta showed up and El Diablo established himself as her father, I had less and less contact with him. I wanted to break entirely, but I gave my word. If he needs me, I'm there. But only if it doesn't interfere with or contradict my loyalties to ExFil, Bones, or Suzie. When I first met him, everyone knew if you were with him, it was for life. If I break clean, he'll be the one to kill me. I'm not afraid of him. I've more than paid my debt to him. But if I'm dead, I can't protect Suzie." He found her again, but she turned her head. "No matter what, I'll always protect her."

"You've put me in a helluva position, Stunner. I can almost understand why you did it. What you should have done was fuckin' come to me! I'd have helped you! As for Suzie, me and the rest of the club have her back. Ain't nobody gettin' through all of us. Not even fuckin' El Diablo."

Stunner nodded. "I hear you." With a heavy heart, he shrugged out of his vest, handing his colors over to Cain. The other man snatched the vest from him without a word.

"I know there's gotta be hell to pay," Stunner said to Cain. "I accept whatever punishment you see fit for betrayal. Even death. Don't give a fuck. I paid my debt to El Diablo, but I gave you the right to my life when I didn't give you a full disclosure. The only thing I ask is that you let me get rid of this assassin hangin' over me. I know you can protect Suzie, but there's a soft hit on her as well." He shook his head. "I can't let this touch her any more than it already has. Let me get rid of this threat. Then my life is yours."

Suzie made a sound, pulling herself together with a shuddering breath. Her father was about to pass judgment on Stunner. She had to know taking a patch away from a member was no small thing. She'd never witnessed it that Stunner was aware of, but she'd certainly heard it talked about. When it happened, it tended to be brutal, even if the club intended to leave the guy alive. For his infraction, Stunner didn't think he'd be that lucky.

Even though Stunner could see by the anguish on her face her heart was in shreds, Suzie made one last stand for him. "Daddy, wait."

"Suzie," Angel started, but Cain waved her off gently.

"Just because he's broken doesn't mean you should throw him away." She turned to Stunner then, still speaking to her father. "And just because I don't believe you should give up on him doesn't mean I'm taking him back. Just means I know how much I owe him. Besides, you can't abandon him now."

Cain gave her an annoyed look. "Well aware of that, baby. We cut him loose, every club who finds out what happened will know they can take us apart one member at a time. So here's what's happenin'. Stunner is still Bones." He tossed the vest back to Stunner. "We take care of our own. To the death. Once this is over and settled to my liking, we'll discuss what to do next."

"I can put this to rights alone," Stunner said. "I fucked it up myself. I can damn well fix it."

"You take one step out that door, Stunner, and I'll shoot you right here. I already owe you a beatin' for breaking my daughter's heart. No matter what happens after this, you're getting the beatdown of your life. Until it's settled, though, we're all in this together."

"Cain, we got company at the main gate requesting entrance." Data checked a tablet he carried, scowling. "Bigass fuckin' limo."

Cain stilled, looking over Stunner's shoulder out the window. "Well Goddamn motherfuck," he swore. "Your buddies are comin' to your rescue, Stunner. Let's go greet them properly, shall we?" As he strode to the door and approached Stunner, Cain lashed out with a left cross, catching Stunner in the jaw.

Stunner grunted, his head snapping to the side. It was by no means Cain's strongest punch. The man had even delivered it with his off hand, but the message was clear. Stunner stood there as each man in Bones took a shot at him as they passed. It wasn't the worst beating he'd ever had, but then they all went easy on him. Still wasn't comfortable by any means. And he was bloodied and sore. The last man to leave the room was Shadow. Stunner winced, but took a breath and stood, hands at his sides.

When Shadow did nothing, Stunner raised an eyebrow, holding his palms up slightly as if to say, "Well? Take your shot."

For long moments Shadow just looked at him. He was a big, intimidating man, heavily muscled and, despite his easy-going manner, was like dynamite when he exploded. He looked ready to explode.

"I trusted you, Stunner. You were my best friend as a kid. Once you came here, I knew you'd changed, but I thought your integrity was still strong. Did I misjudge you?"

"That's for you to decide."

Shadow nodded slowly several times, as if trying to make up his mind what to do. Then, just like Stunner knew he would, Shadow exploded into action. He swung a haymaker at Stunner's head, knocking him to the floor, then he was on him, punching and pounding. Stunner didn't lift a hand to defend himself or to block Shadow. He deserved everything the other man dished out.

Somewhere in the background, he heard a woman's anguished cry, but others stilled her. Then Shadow was off him, stomping away. It took him a while to get his bearings again. Again, not the worst he'd ever taken but he definitely felt it and would for a while. In his heart, he knew he deserved worse. He also knew he'd get worse once this was over.

He groaned as he crawled to his feet, blotting the blood dripping from his nose with his shirt. One of the club girls was there with a towel and a bag of ice. Stunner searched the room for Suzie, not taking the offered items. When he didn't find her, he sighed heavily, taking the towel and ice. He'd lost her. His Suzie. The stinging in his eyes and the way his throat tightened had nothing to do with the beating he'd just received.

Stumbling outside, Stunner came face to face with both El Diablo and El Segador. The Devil and the Reaper. How much torture was he going to have to endure before they just let him die? The waiting was worse than the fucking beatings.

"Ah, there you are, Stunner." El Diablo frowned. "Everything all right?"

Instead of answering, Stunner shrugged.

"You know, you always have a home at Black Reign. No strings. No conditions." Stunner gave him an impatient look, and El Diablo chuckled, raising his hands in surrender. "I'm just making sure you understand. I'll always welcome you with open arms."

"Home is here," Stunner said quietly. "Don't belong anywhere else."

"Well, then," he addressed Cain. "I've come to offer my services. Stunner has an assassin after him. Your daughter as well."

"We can handle this," Cain said, though he looked resigned. Stunner knew they'd be accepting help from Black Reign in some form.

"I've brought my best hunter," El Diablo said with a bright smile. "El Segador --"

"The Reaper. Yeah. We know." Cain sighed. Stunner knew what he was thinking. He didn't want Black Reign anywhere near Bones, but he also needed to know where the other club members were at all times.

"Where are the others?"

El Diablo looked confused. "I brought myself and El Segador. Rycks is here, but he's here as chauffeur. You're welcomed to make use of his talents if you like. I know he helped your sister club in the past. I'm sure Thorn or Vicious can attest to his skills."

"Fuck," Cain muttered, scrubbing a hand through his hair. "Who is the best hunter?"

"Both are equally good," El Diablo said. "But in rural areas, I'd give the edge to El Segador. Reaper was born in Appalachia. He has a feel for the hills. Have you found your prey's region yet?"

"Trackin' him," Data offered, glancing at Cain. "We plan on intercepting him in West Virginia. Know more the closer we get." He glanced at his watch then at Cain.

Cain looked at the Reaper. "Get your shit ready. You'll ride in the cage with Trucker. Make one move I don't much like and I'll take you out myself."

Stunner was surprised at how much relief he felt that Cain had allowed Reaper to join them. Though Reaper was completely loyal to El Diablo, Stunner was willing to bet his life Reaper wouldn't do anything to put any member of Bones at risk without warning Stunner first. He wasn't above killing anyone if necessary, but he wasn't a sociopath. He just marched to the beat of his own moral compass.

"We head out in two hours," Cain said. "That will put us on schedule with our assassin's movements."

"He's being deliberate," Data offered. "His communication suggests he believes Stunner headed back home, but he's not cutting corners. He's investigating places Stunner and/or Suzie visited over the past couple of weeks. Mostly since Stunner showed up at MIT. Still digging into his background, but at least he's methodical."

"Good practice, but makes him easier to track," Reaper muttered.

"My thoughts exactly," Cain said nodding at Reaper. "Stunner, get some sleep. And some ice for your face. You need the rest. Shadow, get Stunner's bike ready. You'll be his wing. You don't take it seriously, you get the same punishment Stunner gets when this is over."

"I'm good, brother. Said my piece."

"Good. We leave in two hours. Mark it… now." Watches set, they all went their separate ways.

Stunner went back inside, hoping to find Suzie, but she wasn't in the common room. One of the club girls, Vanya, approached him. "I think she's done, Stunner. You need company, I'm right here, sugar."

He nodded at the other woman, being polite but knowing that wasn't happening. He'd never touch another woman as long as Suzie was alive. No matter if she took another man or not. Stunner just wasn't built that way.

With a heavy heart, knowing he had work ahead of him, Stunner headed to bed. Sleep came instantly, but not without his own nightmares. Ones of Suzie at the mercy of a shadowy figure Stunner was one step too far away to stop.

Chapter Eight

Helvetia, West Virginia. Population 59. Currently. It was a pretty little place. Stunner hated to mar it with the violence getting ready to happen. The guy they were after called himself Grim. As expected, Reaper took exception. The man actually fit in nicely with Bones. He was as quiet as Stunner remembered, but punctuated moments with a wicked sense of humor. Stunner knew it was all a front, but they all had defense mechanisms.

Grim was staying in a small hunting cabin in the woods. When the group of them staked out the place, they heard him bitching about the accommodations.

"What did the little fucker expect in this area of the country? The fuckin' Four Seasons?" Shadow was pissed. Probably because he was ready for a fucking fight. Not a slaughter.

"We sure he's not the distraction instead of the target?" That was Reaper. Man just shook his head in amazement. Obviously he knew the answer to that question but was so stunned at the stupidity he had to ask.

"Yep," Data said, his voice coming softly from the earpieces they all wore. "That's the man, the myth, the legend. Grim."

"Fuck," Reaper chuckled. "Who the fuck hires someone like this guy?"

"Hey, even assassins gotta start somewhere." Bohannon pulled out his gun with the suppressor attached. "Too bad this one started with this particular job."

Cain just growled. No secret he hated assassins. He stood, obviously seeing enough. "We got the go ahead, Data?" With Data being their eyes and ears -- they'd flown in makeshift surveillance with drones --

he had the final go/no-go. "It's a go. Teach the motherfucker a lesson."

With one mighty kick, Cain splintered the door. Blood winced, shaking his head. The man was normally stoic, but he and Cain thought alike. Likely one of the reasons Cain had brought the man in from Salvation's Bane. He'd made the trip sometime between when Stunner had left to go back to Cambridge and when he'd returned. Good thing, too, because they were going to need his services more than once.

Grim's head whipped around in surprise. He reached for his gun, but Cain was quicker, kicking out again, sending the gun flying and breaking Grim's hand with an audible *crunch*. To his credit, the man didn't scream. Instead, he sprinted across the small room, putting the bed between him and his attackers.

Reaper lunged for the man, snagging him before he could reach the weapon he was going for. He and Bohannon zip-tied his hands and feet, sitting him in one of the hard-backed kitchen chairs. Cain toed another chair around and straddled it, facing the other man head on.

"You the assassin called Grim?"

"No," the guy answered instantly. "Mistaken identity."

Cain snorted. "Well, boys. Looks like we fucked up. Pack it in."

Sword spoke up. "Not sure Data'd want his reputation of having a perfect record tracking motherfuckers ruined. Word gets out… well, I'm not certain his fragile ego can take it."

"Good point," Cain said, never taking his gaze from Grim. "Oh, well, buddy. I tried." He motioned to the rest of the team. "Bunch of hardasses, this lot."

"Look," Grim said. "I'm just doing a job."

"Understood. Don't mean there ain't consequences."

"Just get it over with." The guy sounded defiant but resigned. At least he wasn't a pussy.

"Who sent you?" Cain asked.

"Don't you know?" Grim looked puzzled. "Don't people like you always know the answer to that shit before you ask the question?"

"We do," Cain confirmed. "Just seein' if you tell us the truth."

"Will it make a difference in whether I live or die?"

"No. Will in how hard you die."

Finally, the man went pale, the full impact of what was about to happen hitting him.

"Look. I can give you the name and location of the man who hired me. But you have to let me live if you want it."

"One thing you should know, Grim," Cain said. "Your client got burned. There's no money to pay you."

Grim was silent for long moments, apparently trying to gauge how much truth there was to Cain's statement. Stunner could almost feel sorry for the guy except he had orders to hit Suzie if he could.

"Now. Knowing you got stiffed, is there anything you want to get off your chest?"

Grim closed his eyes. "First fucking job I took," he muttered.

"Why?" Cain said, leaning forward. "Why'd you take this job?"

The other man shrugged. "It was easy money. And a bonus if I could get the girl with my target."

"Do you even know who your fuckin' target is?" Stunner demanded. Hearing him reduce Suzie to a "bonus" set off his rage.

"Some biker dude and his girlfriend." Grim shrugged. "Ugly fucker with his beard and shaggy hair."

Shadow snorted a laugh. "He got you pegged, man. Fugly as sin."

"Shut up, Shadow," Stunner snapped.

Grim's eyes widened. "You?" He glanced around the room. "Which one?"

Stunner stepped forward. "Me, you son of a bitch. Me and my woman. Unfortunately for you, my woman is also his daughter." He pointed to Cain.

"Fuck. Just… fuck." Grim looked defeated. Which was an accurate assessment. "Guy calling himself the Master hired me. Found out his name is Salisberry. Hard to tell, but I think it was the old man's son doing the actual hiring. Nothing concrete on my part. Just things he said. Like him being in school at MIT. I mean, who offers that kind of information? Anyway. For what it's worth, I wouldn't have killed the girl. I wanted the money, but I've never killed a woman."

Cain snorted. "You killed anybody?"

Grim hesitated before sighing and shaking his head.

"Fine," Cain said, standing. "Take him out. Be quick about it."

"Look, what if I promise not to do it again," the guy wheedled. "I'm not a bad person."

"No. You're not. You were just willing to kill someone for money. No questions asked." He paused, looking at the other man. "Sound about right?" When Grim didn't say anything else, Cain continued.

"Assassins have no honor. If you kill someone, it should be about more than just money." He jerked his head, the cue for the rest of them to carry out his orders.

Stunner reached for Grim, but Cain stayed his hand. "No. You're too close. You're here to see it done but you're not doing it."

"If this is for Suzie, that ship's sailed. Ain't nothing of my soul left for her."

"Get the fuck out. Now." Cain was definitely angry. "Get on your fuckin' bike and wait until we're all ready."

Shadow gripped his shoulder and tugged. "Come on, brother. Let them handle this."

Stunner didn't want to. He hated the man on principle. No matter what he said, he knew the man would have killed Suzie if he'd had the chance.

* * *

Their next destination was the Hamptons, New York. Apparently, the Salisberrys were holed up. According to Data, Master's profile had been shut down completely. A bit of work and Data got into the elder Salisberry's security systems in all three houses. He found the pair at the house in the Hamptons.

The father, Markus, had railed at his son day and night for two solid days. Ever since he'd discovered the hit had been placed. Jake sulked, still not getting what the big deal was. Little fucker was about to find out exactly what the big deal was about.

The drive was around nine hours. They drove close to half the distance, then made camp for some rest. Stunner was so tired he hadn't been sure he could keep going until they stopped, but knew better than to whine. Especially after everything that had happened. Shadow kept him engaged during the ride, keeping him awake. Probably saved his life during that four-hour ride. But Stunner would have laid the bike down rather than ask Cain to stop.

The second camp was set up, Stunner lay back and closed his eyes...

He woke when Shadow gently shook his shoulder. "Up, brother. Time to get moving."

It wasn't full dark, but by the time they got on the road it would be. He glanced at his watch. Holy fuck! He'd slept close to twelve hours? Yeah. He'd been on his last leg, but, judging by the stiffness in his body, he hadn't moved the entire time.

"Got close to another five hours to go," Shadow said. "You good?"

"Fuck," Stunner said, stretching out the kinks in his back. "Didn't realize I was such a pussy."

Shadow snorted. "I always knew, but don't worry. You hide it well."

"Listen up," Cain said over the chatter in the camp as they broke it apart. "Once we get there, the house is surrounded by a wooded area. Don't expect undergrowth so going should be easy. Remember to cover your tracks. The property has a main house and a guest house. A smaller pool house is just off the guest house. Data says they're staying in the guest house. Apparently, Markus thinks he'll have advance notice, that any enemy will break into the main house and he'll hear the alarm. There's a good chance we take them with little resistance."

"You got a plan? Killin' 'em in The Hamptons ain't gonna go unnoticed." Shadow crossed his arms over his chest.

"Always got a plan." Cain stood, reaching for his helmet. "If there's no more questions?" When no one said anything, he nodded. "Let's ride, brothers."

* * *

Getting into the Salisberrys' pool house took little doing. Data disabled the security on the whole property, and Jake was asleep. Markus had gone to the kitchen for a Scotch before heading to bed himself, and that was when Cain approached him.

"The best thing you can do for yourself and your son right now is to keep quiet," Cain said mildly. He sat at the table, much like he had when questioning Grim. The chair had been turned around backwards and his arms were resting on the back. The rest of Bones were in various places around the room, including in Jake's bedroom. The young man had yet to wake up and none of the men in Bones were making an effort to wake him. Not yet. His time would come, though, Stunner thought.

"Who are you people? My house is hooked up to the 911 center. The second you broke in a silent alarm went off over there. The cops will be here soon."

"That might be true," Cain said, still mild, "if our tech guy hadn't disabled the entire system. No one's coming to help you. You're at our mercy." Cain shrugged. "Or lack thereof."

"If this is about what Jake did, I can assure you, he's learned his lesson. No one got hurt. No harm, no foul." Markus chuckled nervously. "Right?"

"You're sure there was no harm? Because the contract was picked up."

Markus's face paled. "So, the girl's dead?"

"No," Stunner supplied, taking his cue from Cain. When he nodded, Stunner continued. "But the girl in question is my woman. And his daughter." He pointed at Cain who looked cold as death. "Not something either of us is willing to let slide."

There was a silence that stretched on until Stunner was certain Salisberry would break down and cry, begging them to spare his life. "So," the man finally asked. "What happens now?"

"Now," Cain said, taking out a glass vial and a syringe. "You're going to inject yourself with insulin. Quick. Painless. You die, but you get off easy."

"And if I refuse?"

"You still die. Just not as easy," Stunner said. "And your son lasts for weeks instead of a few hours."

"Hours? *Hours*? You're talking about torture! You can't do that!"

"Same as you can't put a hit out on someone just because they're in your way," Cain said immediately. He stood slowly, leaning in so that he was looking directly into Salisberry's eyes. "Same as you can't kill my daughter just because your son is a fucking dumb fuck!"

"I didn't put the hit on your daughter! And I cut it off as soon as I found out about it! Everything worked out for the best!"

"What about the daughter of your business partner? When he thought you were taking the company you'd both built from the ground up in the wrong direction and fought you on it? Did that 'work out for the best' as well?" The man swallowed but said nothing. "That's what I thought. You're not so innocent. Are you?" Cain nodded to the vial. "I'll be happy to help you if you like."

"Why can't you let Jake go this way, too? Why do you have to torture him?"

"Because he put a hit out on my friend and my daughter out of *spite*." Now, Cain was showing the true anger Stunner knew he hid well most of the time. "He's a lazy little fucker who got called out by Stunner when he tried to intimidate her and threatened her in her own home. When that didn't work, and he pissed himself in front of God and everybody, he decided it was better to kill the pair of them." Cain tilted his head. "I'm sorry you raised a goddamned monster, but that ain't my problem, you son of a bitch. Now get busy." He nodded to the syringe and glass vial. "Or I'll take it as a refusal, and you can go to your deaths together. Watch each other as we skin you a-*fuckin'*-live!"

Markus Salisberry didn't argue anymore. He wrote the note of apology Cain instructed. He made sure Salisberry's ex-wife was taken care of just because the man objected so much. Then he injected himself with as much insulin as he could get out of the vial. The Bones members waited until Cain was satisfied the elder Salisberry was dead, then they turned their attention on Jake Salisberry. They had him tied and gagged. Made getting him out of New York easier. Again, West Virginia was the target destination.

This time, Cain allowed Stunner to participate. Probably because, though Jake could be traced back to Stunner and Suzie, they had a plan in place to get rid of his body permanently.

The beating lasted for three hours. Cain and Stunner took turns while the rest of Bones bore witness. No one said anything, even when Jake started pleading for his life. Then for them to end it. When Jake's bladder finally let go, Cain nodded to Stunner. Stunner took out the silenced, clean .45, took aim at the back of Jake's head, and pulled the trigger.

"El Segador. You're a hunter," Cain said, shaking out his arms. Stunner knew the feeling. The beating had been a brutal one. Even though they'd used more than just their fists, Stunner's arms felt like lead weights.

"I am."

"You good at finding places to hide a body?"

"In this area?" He shrugged. "Sure. I know more than my fair share. All of them one-hundred percent."

"Blood, stay with our good friend Reaper. The two of you are in charge of cleaning. Bohannon, you'll supervise. I want no evidence anywhere of what happened to this fuck. As far as the world is concerned, he simply disappeared."

"You got it, boss," Bohannon said, giving Cain a two-fingered salute. The three of them went to work while the rest of Bones left for the camp. Bohannon, Blood, and Reaper would meet them as soon as the mess was taken care of.

Shadow, again, was at Stunner's side the whole ride back to camp. The wait for the others was one of the longest of Stunner's life.

Stunner had time to reflect on everything that had happened. The only thing he really regretted was not telling Cain and Shadow everything up front. By not doing so, he knew he'd betrayed their trust in the worst way. Had he been straight with them, he'd be headed home to Suzie right now instead of awaiting his sentence. Well, whatever Cain decided, he'd take it like a man. For the offenses of spying and continuing to be in contact with El Diablo he more than deserved it, even if he'd refused to give the other man anything of substance. The result of those crimes had broken Suzie's heart, and there was no punishment harsh enough to make up for that.

It was a couple of hours before the three men emerged from the woods into the camp. They were in a different part of West Virginia now, but it was no less secluded, just several hundred miles away from the last location.

When the bikes were turned off and everyone sat around the fire, Cain addressed them.

"Been a long, hard ride, brothers. I want you to know I appreciate what you did for Suzie. In this whole fuckin' mess, she's the only one who's truly innocent." He pinned Stunner with his piercing gaze. "We have one more mess to clean up before we can go home." Stunner opened his mouth to tell him to do his worst, but Cain held up a hand. "I'm gonna keep this simple, Stunner. I ain't gonna kill you, though I won't lie. I considered it. Strongly."

Stunner didn't blame the man. He'd been the one to bring El Diablo right to the fucking front door. While the man wasn't evil, El Diablo would always be out for El Diablo, or, perhaps, his daughter, Magenta. He would never have the interest of his own club at heart, let alone the interests of another club.

"What I am gonna do is beat your ass. You knew it was comin', so you should be prepared. Trucker will take care of your bike, and you'll ride in the back of the cage when we're done. Anything to say before this starts?"

"If it goes further than you intend, make sure Suzie gets all my shit. Ain't much, but it's hers."

"Understood," Cain acknowledged.

Then the beating commenced…

* * *

Stunner had no idea where they were. All he knew was that he felt like every single bone in his body had been broken. Twice. He tried not to groan at every bump in the road, but, honestly, he was certain Cain had made a pact with Trucker to hit every single pothole there was.

They'd been kind enough to give him some ice for the swelling on his face, but he was definitely wishing he hadn't shaved the beard. He'd have had something to hide behind, at least. For most of the ride, he'd lain in the back seat. He knew, though, as they got closer to Kentucky, he needed to pull himself together. No matter how much he was hurting, he would not ride back to the clubhouse in a fuckin' cage when there was nothing wrong with his fuckin' bike.

They stopped just inside the border of Pulaski County. Still nearly forty-five minutes from home, but it was a big fuckin' county. The door to the truck opened. Cain stood there assessing him.

"Not as pretty as you once were."

"Nothin' my fuckin' beard won't cover."

"You good enough to ride?" Cain's face was blank. He sounded like he could give two shits but felt obligated to ask the question.

"Take more than a beatin' to keep me off my bike in my home territory."

Cain nodded. "Good. Hop to it."

Stunner unloaded his bike, taking his time so he could get his legs back under him. No one rushed him. Once he climbed on, he sat up straight, eyes up and on the road.

"Stunner," Cain called, approaching him. "You forgot something."

Cain tossed Stunner his colors, the vest he'd stowed in the truck. It had lain folded carefully on the seat beside him. Though Cain had given it back, insisting he keep it, Stunner hadn't thought he'd ever wear it again.

"You wear those colors. Wear them with your brothers." He took a step closer, close enough he was right in Stunner's face. "And while we're on the way to the clubhouse, you better be fuckin' thinkin' 'bout what you're gonna say to Suzie. Get down on your fuckin' knees if you have to, but you will make this right with her. You will grovel at her feet until she forgives you, then you will convince her to wear your fuckin' property patch. Otherwise, we'll revisit this."

Stunner couldn't help himself. He chuckled. Then he laughed. Then he outright guffawed. To his surprise, Cain joined him before leaning in to hug Stunner. He clapped him on the back several times. Stunner couldn't help the yelp of pain because he was still laughing. He discovered it was much harder to stifle his shrieks of pain when he was just trying to keep quiet that it was when he was already making noise.

"Fuckin' bastard," Stunner half laughed, half groaned. "You fuckin' did that on purpose."

"Not denying it. Now. Let's get home."

Chapter Nine

Suzie hadn't come out of her room since Stunner left. First, she knew Vanya had offered herself to him, but Suzie had no idea if he'd accepted. She'd been too hurt and shocked out of her mind to investigate. Or even to find a gun and shoot Vanya. Whether or not Vanya had been successful in getting into Stunner's bed would determine if Stunner got to live.

Angel had come to her several times, but she couldn't get the comfort she needed from her mother. In the end, she just stuck a "Leave Me the Fuck Alone" sign on the door and locked it. Then proceeded to have a good cry. Over several hours. Then she managed to doze off.

When she woke, it was to the scent of Stunner…

And blood.

"What the hell?" Suzie sat straight up, shoving herself back and away from the big man sitting on the edge of her bed. It took her a moment to realize it was, in fact, Stunner. He wasn't talking to her because his face was so swollen she knew it had to hurt to talk.

"Holy shit! Stunner!" She tried to climb out of bed but he shook his head. Then winced. "What happened? Are you OK? What am I saying? *Of course you're not OK!*" Despite his protests, she got out of bed and ran to the bathroom, wetting a cloth and coming back. She urged him to lie down, and she washed the blood from his face.

"You should see the other guy," he finally croaked out. One thing she noticed was that he was still wearing his vest. His colors. Bones colors.

"Dad let you stay in?"

"Yeah. Gotta make things right with you." Man sounded half dead.

"Not sure that's happening, Stunner. You lied to me."

He sighed under her ministrations, actually leaning into her touch. Which did nothing to melt her resolve. At fucking all. Right.

"I never lied, baby. I just didn't tell you the whole truth."

"You're splitting hairs," she snapped. He winced when she was less than careful over a nasty bump on his temple. "Sorry," she muttered, ashamed she'd taken out her pain and irritation on him when he was obviously hurting.

"You're right. I just… I didn't know how to start. I can honestly tell you that when I came to Bones, I never intended to do anything other than to watch out for you and the boys. I used every excuse I could think of to get El Diablo to agree to me going. But I did it to make sure all of you were safe."

She looked at him. *Really* looked at him. "You're telling the truth, aren't you?"

"Suzie, I can't lose you. Not as a friend. Not as my woman." He gently grabbed her wrist and moved her hand away from his face. Turning slightly to face her, he winced a little but pulled her to him. "Please, Suz." He reached for her hand and brought it to his mouth. Which was busted so he winced, but still kissed her palm. "I need you. I'll always need you."

She was in so much trouble. "I shouldn't give in to you. You broke my heart, Stunner."

"I know, baby. I deserved everything I got here and more for what I did to you. But I'm telling you now, I have no more secrets. The only thing I have left to tell you is that I love you. With everything inside me, Suz, I love you."

She sucked in a breath. "I love you, too." The words just tripped out before she could stop them.

His brow wrinkled. "You do?"

"Yeah, baby. I love you, too." Then the full meaning of what he'd said hit her. "Wait. What do you mean you deserved everything you got and more?"

"Your dad was less than impressed with the things I kept from you. Think he was more upset that you didn't know all that shit than he was about not knowing it himself. Not sure I've ever had a beatin' so bad. Woulda been worse except we'd both already worn ourselves out."

"He what?"

"He only did what had to be done. Shoulda killed me."

"He most certainly should not have! What the shit, Stunner?"

"Don't mean to be grouchy, but could we talk about this another time?"

Her heart melted a little. This was her Stunner. He was trying to be stoic through the whole beating thing, but he was hurting and, with her, he didn't care to show it.

"Of course. I'll just mark it on the calendar. We'll pick this up in a couple days."

He snorted, then groaned. "Thanks."

"Strip. I need to see where else you're hurt. Then I'll get whatever I need from Mama. We'll have you better in no time."

"You know the rules, Suz. I'll get naked if you get naked."

Grinning, she said, "Deal. But only after I check you over." When he reached for her, she added in a stern voice. "And *only* if I think you're up for it."

"Oh, baby, I'm definitely up for it."

Of course he was. "Stunner, you're half dead."

"Take more than being half dead for me not to be up for this task." He tugged her to him and into his arms. He buried his nose in her neck and inhaled deeply. "Fuck, I've missed you!"

"I've missed you, too." She sniffed, then wiped her eyes briskly, needing to get back to the task at hand. "Enough stalling. Strip and lay down."

He chuckled, holding his ribs as he did so. She went back to the bathroom to get some antiseptic and bandages. It wasn't much, but it would do until Mama could look him over. When she returned, he was stark naked, laid out on her bed like a masculine buffet for one. His cock was pointed due north.

"Wow," she said. "Guess you are up for the task."

"Can't say I didn't warn you, baby."

She just shook her head. Stunner was covered from head to toe in red and blue bruises. The only cuts were on his face, and they didn't look too bad. Suzie took her time, being as thorough as she could. She wanted to think it was to make sure he wasn't really injured, but, though that was a big part of it, she wanted to run her hands over his body. To get that naughty thrill she got whenever she touched him.

Every time her hands stroked over his skin, muscles jumped to her touch. He growled several times, but never pushed her away. At first, she thought she was hurting him. She'd drawn back and made her touch lighter, but he'd quickly dispelled that notion when he pressed down hard on her hands with his. The groan he gave her then was of pure masculine satisfaction.

"You like it when I touch you?" Suzie could remember a time when she'd never have dared ask that question. But this was Stunner. *Her* Stunner. She could do anything she wanted with him and never be embarrassed. First, she knew he'd let her try anything she wanted. Second, even if he didn't like it, he'd still let her explore. If she liked it, he might just let her have her way with him until he learned to like it. Stunner would never judge or make fun of her. He was her man. Her protector. Her lover.

"Fuck no, I don't like it." He grinned. "I fuckin' *love* it!"

"Shithead," she muttered, though she was doing her best not to giggle.

"Yeah, but I'm your shithead."

"Oh really." Suzie gave him her best coquettish grin. "If you're mine, that means I can do this" -- she lowered her mouth to his cock, never taking her gaze from his --"and you couldn't stop me. You know. Because you're mine."

He swallowed. "You wouldn't."

To show him she most definitely would, she opened her mouth and ever so slowly took him inside.

* * *

Stunner's hips nearly came off the fucking bed. He gave a shout, then winced when everything hurt. Holy shit! In his wildest imaginings, he'd never once thought he'd be able to get her to go down on him. He wasn't complaining -- he was just surprised. Her past experience in this area wasn't pleasant. But as long as she was enjoying herself, he wasn't arguing.

Her mouth was hot, her tongue a living thing over his cock. She sucked and pulled, moving over him in a silken glide. Her hair tickled his thighs, adding to the sensation she effortlessly built in him. Never once did she take her gaze from his. He wanted to lie there and just relax and enjoy, but there was no way in fuck he was missing this sight. Propping himself up on his elbows, Stunner watched her take him deep into her mouth. Her throat muscles tried to milk him of his cum, but he was determined to hold off.

"Fuck, Suz. Just... *fuck*!"

"Mmmmm." She moaned around him, moving faster and faster. He knew she was going to bring him off, but he wasn't sure she was ready.

"Suz, I'm gonna come! Pull back! Pull back!"

To his utter surprise and ultimate delight, she just gripped his hips, her nails biting deep. The little sting was enough to send Stunner over the edge. With a brutal shout, he shot his load deep inside her mouth. She swallowed every drop, moaning and milking him with her hand.

When it was over, he was in no way satiated. He wanted more. He just wasn't ready to admit she might have been right. His body was beaten to shit.

She slid from between his legs and moved up to lie beside him, shedding her clothing as she went. Stunner braced himself to give her whatever she needed, but all she did was pull a quilt lying at the bottom of the bed over them.

"What're you doin'?" he asked, genuinely perplexed.

"Sleeping with you."

"Thought you wanted... you know."

"Sex? To make love with you?" She grinned up at him, leaning in to kiss his chin. "I do. But you'll still be here when you heal a bit. I have no intention of letting you leave this bed for a very long while. Maybe not even then."

"I've got to give you the vest I had made for you. Gotta do it in front of everyone. Especially your dad."

Her face darkened. "Don't talk to me about my dad right now. I'm kinda pissed at him."

"Huh? What for?"

"For this! I can't believe he beat you up!"

Stunner chuckled. "Suz, he wants us together. Knowing your dad, it was for two reasons. He was genuinely angry with me. But if that had been it, he'd have just expelled me from Bones. Coulda killed me, but I don't think he would have. At least, not for this. He believed that I didn't compromise ExFil or Bones in any way."

The door opened and Cain walked in, frowning to see the two of them in bed. Then he scrubbed a hand over his face. "Fuck. Stunner... Goddamn. Really? Didn't I beat you enough? Do I need to get Torpedo in here to finish the job?"

"Dad! Get out of my bedroom!"

"Honey, this is Stunner's bedroom. You just took it over when we left. Angel told me that. This is the Bones clubhouse, and I'm the president. I can go anywhere I fuckin' want." Though Stunner thought he looked like he wanted to be anywhere but in that room at the moment. Not that Stunner blamed him. Talk about awkward! "Besides, I just wanted to make sure you two were patching things up."

"We are," Stunner said.

"Until you walked in, that is," Suzie muttered. Stunner just chuckled and pulled her closer.

"You're welcome, by the way," Cain said to Stunner with a wry grin. "Looks like the beating worked."

There was a moment of silence. Then Suzie reached for a pillow and threw it at Cain. "You're a pig! Does Mom know about this side of you? That's barbaric! What if you'd really hurt him?"

"Honey, he's not gonna hurt me that bad."

"Says the man in bed with *my daughter*."

"Bad timing there." Stunner shrugged.

"Just get out. We're fine. Once Stunner is healed, he's going to present me with his property patch in front of the whole club. Satisfied?"

"Completely," Cain said, then left, shutting the door behind him.

"You are. Aren't you?" Suzie sounded unsure of herself now that Cain was gone and she was alone with him once more.

"Are what? Giving you my property patch?" When she nodded, Stunner squeezed her tightly. Without wincing at all. "Honey, just try and stop me. Ain't askin' you to take it either. I'm just gonna put the fuckin' thing on you and tell everyone you're mine. Everyone else, stay the fuck away."

"Don't think I didn't notice you don't seem to be hurting as much as you were letting on. I did."

"Well, I might've exaggerated. Just a little. Ain't sayin' my body don't hurt like a motherfucker, just sayin', when it comes to you, I'll use everything I can to keep you."

"Well. I guess when you put it like that."

Stunner couldn't help but chuckle. "God, I fuckin' love you, baby."

"I love you, too. You think El Diablo will leave you alone now?"

He sighed. "I don't know, baby. I doubt it. But I think he's changed. There was something different about him. Maybe finding his daughter truly has mellowed him out."

"I guess we'll just have to keep an eye on him."

"I'm sure Data has it covered."

"If he doesn't, I can assure you that I will. I'm not letting him take you from me, Stunner. Not El Diablo. Not anyone."

"Ain't no one gonna separate us ever again, Suz. I swear it."

"Me too. We're in this together."

"Forever."

Havoc (Salvation's Bane MC 4)
Marteeka Karland

Spring -- The father of my child is pressing for custody. Which is how I ended up dancing at Salvation's Angels, a strip club owned by the notorious Salvation's Bane MC. I have to earn enough to pay my attorney, then I'm out of here. I have enough on my plate without having to deal with the sexy-as-sin vice president of Salvation's Bane. But Havoc, the bastard, wants me to stay. He's found another way for me to make enough money to pay my bills, but I'm not sure he's got my best interests in mind.

Havoc -- It's a pisser of a bad day. My son would have been sixteen today, had he lived. On my way to drown my sorrows I came across Spring, swishing her little ass on stage at our strip club. She's not naked yet, but with that body and the way she moves, I don't want other men seeing what she's got to offer. There's a loophole in every contract. Three songs. With me. After that? Well, I just hope my indecent proposal doesn't push her away. At least, not until I'm ready for her to go. One problem. Now I'm addicted to her and the feisty son she's raising. I know I'll do whatever it takes to keep them safe. And make them both mine.

Chapter One

"Place is really lit tonight." Stryker grinned.

Havoc glanced at him over his coffee cup and grunted. Tonight wasn't the night for this. He knew where Stryker was going.

"Girls are smokin' hot."

"I'm not interested in the girls, Stryker. Here to make sure things run smoothly."

"Yeah. But you got to admit --" As he spoke, a busty waitress brushed her tits against first Stryker then Havoc as she set two cups of coffee on the table in front of them. She winked and bumped Havoc with her hip as she stepped away. "Makin' things run smoothly should have a few perks with it."

Stryker was yanking Havoc's chain. Trying to get a rise out of his brother. Havoc knew it. Appreciated it. The man was his oldest friend, and he knew when Havoc was in one of his moods. On this day, he was always in a bad mood. Today was the seventh anniversary of the day his ex-wife gave him divorce papers. Not exactly noteworthy in itself, but she'd done it deliberately to hurt him. Because she could never stand not being the center of attention.

She'd had him served on the first anniversary of his son's death.

Yeah. Today was not the day.

"Back off, Stryker."

"Well, why the fuck not? Get some pussy. Pick out any of the girls. No one will reject you, you know that. Get laid hard. You'll feel better."

"I said," he snarled, finally meeting Stryker's gaze, "Back the fuck off."

Stryker put his hands in the air in surrender. "Fine, man. But at least let me take over guard duty. I'll get Dazz and Beaner to help. They've been doing very well keeping the guys under control without being all flashy and pushy. You need something more than that fuckin' coffee. You're like a bear with a sore paw."

"Fuck you too, asshole."

Stryker just chuckled. "I'll take that as a yes. Get on up to your office. Or better yet, check out the new girl on tier two. Babe's a looker."

Havoc grunted again. Yeah. He'd just get right on that. If he wanted to fuck, he'd go to the Playground, a BDSM club Salvation's Bane owned, and find a willing sub to scene with. No names. No expectations other than a fucking good time. Best of all, no fucking strings. And no fucking talking if he didn't want to fucking talk.

No. He wasn't in the right frame of mind. Even the masochists wouldn't appreciate him tonight.

The bass from the music pulsed through his body, making him slightly ill whereas he normally enjoyed the rhythmic pulse. Salvation's Angels boasted the most beautiful girls in the Palm Beach area, due in no small part to the fact that they were paid very well. Thumping bass pounding through the body enhanced the eroticism of the place, adding the sensation of touch mostly denied otherwise. The club might be owned by a biker club, but they served only the best liquor, the best food, in an environment that was more like a dance club than a strip club. While there were girls performing on stage, there was also a dance floor for guests and, if one paid enough, the girls would dance with the patrons. It was difficult to monitor everyone, but Havoc only hired the best security. There were several men tasked only with keeping an eye on the dance floor, and they were fucking good at their jobs.

Angels had two tiers and three levels. The first floor was for the general public. Alcohol was served, and there was a dance floor, but the girls kept their thongs on and didn't dance with patrons. Lap dances were given in a strictly monitored "private" section, but that floor was more like a standard strip club.

Tier two was for the more "robust" patrons -- meaning men or women who would pay top dollar for food, drink, and women. While sex was still strictly prohibited, these customers were given more leeway in their experiences. The women, while completely nude, still called the shots. They were allowed to pull back if they felt threatened or touched in a way that made them fear they'd crossed the line. Obviously, anything that made them uncomfortable was allowed to be shut down, too. Most had as much fun as the patrons did. The only thing not allowed was penetration of any kind. And not a single thong in sight.

Stryker was right. Havoc could have his pick of beautiful women. More than one of them were club girls of Salvation's Bane. A couple in particular he knew could take his mind from the harsh memories surrounding this day.

Fuck. Who was he kidding? The rage was too close. Nothing but a good knock-down-drag-out was going to make a dent in his state of mind today.

A deafening round of cheers came from the second tier stage, pulling Havoc out of his dark musings. He'd been on his way to the third floor, where the offices were located. Naturally, his head turned in the direction of the uproar…

And he stopped in his fucking tracks.

On the stage was a vision straight out of his most erotic fantasies. Dressed in an intricately strapped black outfit that left her tits bare while surrounding them with those fucking straps that also crisscrossed her body. Thigh-high boots were garnished in chrome chains, as was the rest of the fucking outfit. Long, long black tresses gleamed blue in the stage lighting with every move she made. Though her outfit covered a good bit, it revealed a healthy portion of gleaming pale skin. She was like some kind of dark angel out of his dreams. She had a deceptively innocent look in her eyes, but her body and that outfit told another story.

And the woman could dance like sin on a stick...

She had this thing she could do with her hips, snapping side to side and front to back. Like a belly dance or some shit. Subtle but deliberate. Whatever it was, it was erotic as hell. And she did it to Metallica. *Fuck*.

Instead of continuing on to his office, Havoc found himself rooted to the spot, mesmerized by the pale beauty. And just exactly when had he taken a step toward the stage? And why had he dug out bills from his pockets, and why was he reaching for her even now?

The string of the thong at her hips was already stuffed full of dollar bills, as was nearly every strap on the outfit, and she'd been on stage less than half a song. God, he wanted to touch her! Wanted his lips around the pouty nipples she'd bared. On what he just knew would be a bare little cunt. His mouth *watered* for a taste of her, for Christ's sake! When she swished her hips in his direction, that maddening snapping action making the bills in the band of her thong flutter like a skirt, Havoc nearly fell to the floor and worshiped at her feet. All those long, gleaming blue/black locks played along her bare ass, just giving him a glimpse of her pale cheeks. Yeah, he wanted his mouth there too.

As if in a trance, he found himself tucking a hundred-dollar bill into the strap at the front of her hip. Daringly close to no-man's-land. She gave him a sharp glance in reprimand, but said nothing. Only shimmied her hips to shake him free. To anyone watching, it would look like she was just moving, but Havoc knew she was keeping him from touching where he shouldn't.

And why the fuck did she have on a fucking thong in the first Goddamned place? A body like hers should never be covered. Unless it was by a man.

No. Not just a man. *Him.*

With a decisive shake of his head, Havoc tried to power through what felt like a trance. When was the last time a woman affected him this much? Had one ever? As he watched her dance, he was aware that all eyes in the place were on her. Probably thirty naked women in the room, but the only one clothed -- sort of -- was the one who had everyone's attention. And it sent a flush of pure, unadulterated rage through Havoc.

She circled her hips as she spun slowly with each turn. Her arms above her head lifted her ripe breasts encased in those leather straps. God, he wanted to suck one of those tempting peaks into his mouth. He'd make the nipple pebble under his tongue and teeth. He'd suck until she held him to her, crying out in pure ecstasy.

When she walked down the short runway in the middle of the crowded stage area and reached the pole, she gave a little hop and grabbed the thing, hooking her leg and swinging around and around. The men surrounding her went fucking *wild*.

Where the fuck had this girl come from? When had they hired her? *Who* had hired her? Havoc normally did the hiring because he wasn't a pushover. He didn't bring in girls who were looking to get into the club or lay a biker. He hired girls who could bring in the money and keep it as professional as a stripper possibly could. Some of the other guys in Salvation's Bane weren't so discriminatory. So where had she come from?

When her song was over, she was still fucking dressed. Well, except for her tits poking through the leather straps.

Havoc gritted his teeth, clenching his fists when more and more men shoved bills into her boot and various straps along her body. Anywhere they could tuck a bill without getting kicked out and still touch that silky-looking skin. No, fuck "silky looking". It was baby soft. He could still feel it on the backs of his fingers where he'd tucked his own damned bill.

The second her song was over, she turned and twisted her luscious ass as she exited the stage. It wasn't a retreat, exactly, but Havoc got the impression she didn't want to be there a moment longer. Or maybe it was wishful thinking. The money the club paid was good, but what she'd just had shoved at her was well worth the three minutes on stage with a bunch of loud, rowdy men. At least, that's what he heard the girls say backstage. And this girl had taken back nearly double what he'd seen other girls get.

Fuck. Now he had to go to the dressing room and see who she was. Because there was no way she was getting out of this club tonight without him knowing everything there was to know about her.

He reached for his phone and texted Stryker.

Who hired the fuckin new girl?

There was about a minute before the other man answered. *Think it was Beast. Favor to his ol' lady.*

OK. That was different.

Since when do we do favors?

Since when do you send texts?

This was the reason Havoc hated text messages. No way to properly convey his annoyance at someone calling him out about hating text messages in the first place. The music was so fucking loud there was no way a phone call would work, and he wasn't leaving this area until he'd talked to the woman.

Not asking again. He also hated texting because his fingers were too fucking big for the buttons. Of course, auto correct was in his favor. Some of the time.

Since Beast said hire her.

Havoc stomped away from the stage, headed to the dressing room. This had catastrophe written all over it. If there was trouble, the cops might come investigating. Havoc would not have that. Salvation's Angels was his club to manage. That included the hiring of dancers. He'd visit this with Beast tonight at the clubhouse. The man might be the club's enforcer, but Havoc was the fucking vice president, and just as big and mean as Beast.

Inside the dressing room, the women were talking and giggling. Some were adorning their bodies with glitter and shimmering lotion. Others were adding body jewelry to their nipples. A couple were adding clips to their pussies that had little dangling gems that drew the eye when they moved. One was easing a fucking jeweled butt plug inside her. Normally, the sight would have at least given Havoc a passing hard on, but now it just annoyed him. Mainly because the woman he was looking for was actually dressed. Like in shorts and a T-shirt dressed.

She had stacked her money neatly and had just wrapped what looked like a hair tie around it when he entered. One young woman saw him and let out an excited squeal. Despite the situation, Havoc couldn't help but grin. Glitter -- yes, that was her real name -- dashed across the room and jumped at him, throwing herself into his arms and wrapping her lithe arms and legs around him tightly.

"Havoc! I've missed you so much!"

He chuckled. "Darlin', you just saw me last night."

"I know! Still missed you!" She untangled herself from him and slid to the floor gracefully. "Did you see my performance?"

"Sorry, squirt. Missed it this time. But you know I'll catch your next one. I never miss more than one a week."

She pouted prettily, but still leaned up and pecked his cheek with her lips. "Fine. But, just for that, next time Stryker wants to dance with me you have to let him."

Havoc sighed. "You know that's not happenin'."

Instead of pouting or trying to change his mind, she just giggled and shrugged. "Can't blame a girl for trying."

"Well, quit working here. Then you can dance with him all you want. You know the rules."

"No fraternizing with management. Yeah. But it shouldn't apply to me. I'm special," she said brightly.

"That you are, darlin', but the rules still apply to you."

"Well, I like Stryker, but a girl's gotta make a living." She didn't look like she was too broken up about it. Not that she was fickle or anything. Glitter just liked having a good time. And she was one of the best dancers in the club. She brought in customers and never caused trouble.

"You happen to know the new girl?" Havoc nodded in the direction of the woman in question.

"Spring? Yeah. She's really cool. Sweet, too. Did you see her moves? She can actually belly dance! That is so freaking awesome! She's gonna teach me, and we're going to dance together. Except I won't have on clothes." She gave Havoc another megawatt smile. "Though, I gotta admit, that outfit she has is killer."

"Her name's Spring?" Havoc must have let his amusement show because Glitter frowned at him for the first time he could remember.

"Yeah. So?"

Havoc raised his hands. "Nothing, darlin'. It's a nice name."

Glitter narrowed her eyes. "You better not say anything to her about it." That was new. No if/then clause attached. Like, the very thought of him displeasing Glitter was threat enough. Unfortunately, it kind of was. If he made Glitter mad, or, God forbid, hurt her feelings, Havoc was man enough to admit he couldn't take on the whole club. And that was what he'd be facing. Glitter might not be a club girl, but she was loved by every single member of Salvation's Bane because of her winning personality and complete and utter honesty in everything she did.

"You gonna introduce us?"

Glitter looked at him a long time. Then she shook her head. "Nope. Because I'm not going to be responsible when you act like a horse's ass." Then she flounced off back to her dressing table to finish slathering shimmering lotion over her skin. Havoc tried not to chuckle again but couldn't manage it. Too much effort for something that was funny as shit. Girl had him pegged. And his bad-boy image was completely lost on her. She was affectionate with her friends and a touchy-feely kind of person, but she had never once shown real interest in any of the guys in the club, something not all of the girls at Angels could attest to.

With a last glance at Glitter, Havoc made his way to the woman he really wanted to see. As she stuffed makeup, towels, and her outfit into a large duffel, he cleared his throat to announce his presence. Spring stiffened, standing up straight. She took a deep breath before turning around, her shoulders rising and falling as she did. When she turned toward him, the full impact of her deep sapphire eyes hit him like a sucker punch to the balls. So much so that he nearly doubled over. A sharp grunt left him before he could prevent it, and he knew he was in real trouble.

"Can I help you?" Her voice was magical. Like tinkling bells or some shit. It was clear and smooth, but pitched high, like she was very young.

"You leaving?" The very idea of her not being here for the rest of the night made him want to growl in displeasure.

"Yes. Fleur told me she'd get me one dance. I did it, so I'm leaving."

Havoc's eyes narrowed. "What do you mean, one dance? You didn't sign a contract?"

"I -- Oh, yes. I did. I just… It's a one-time thing. I needed money fast, and this was the best way to go about it. Fleur said Beast approved it." She dug into her bag and pulled her copy of the contract all the dancers at the club signed. When she handed it to him, he noted her hand trembling. Nervous?

He took it from her and noted the changes done in Beast's handwriting. It was also signed by the vice president as well as Thorn. The most notable changes were that she didn't have to stage dance completely nude, and she didn't get paid by the club. Only collected her tips. Also, the section that noted the time she was to spend on the club for standard wages was the minimum. One hour. Which was where he was going to be a bastard.

"You've only spent three minutes on stage." He tapped the page with a finger. "You've contracted for one hour."

Her mouth opened, and she seemed to struggle for words. "I -- b-but Fleur said I c-could just do one d-dance."

"You're a good draw, girl. Need you out there at least a couple more times tonight." As Havoc spoke, Spring started breathing rapidly, and sweat broke out over her body.

"I-I can't. I o-only brought one outfit. I only have one dance ready."

Yeah. He was going to hell in a big way. He was the biggest bastard in the world, but he was about to propose an alternative. He was also acutely aware of the girls in the dressing room watching them intently.

"I see. Well, I can offer an alternative."

If anything, she seemed to be even more nervous. "W-what's that?"

"You said you needed money fast. Did you make all you needed?" He pointed to her bag where she'd stuffed the bound bills she'd counted out."

She shrugged. "I'm not sure. I just stacked them and put a band around them. I'll count it later."

"If you're not sure, then do you want to hear my offer?"

He could see she didn't. Spring nibbled her bottom lip, thinking over the situation. Havoc could see she was hesitant, but must need the money pretty badly. Finally, her shoulders slumped, and she shrugged, answering softly, "Yes, please."

Havoc raised his eyebrow. The girl sounded almost defeated. A small part of Havoc wanted to ask how much she needed and just give her the fucking money. He had plenty. He could part with whatever she needed and probably never miss it. But there was that ruthless side of him that was a selfish bastard. He wanted close to this girl and would take her any way he could.

"Three dances on the floor. With a patron. Three dances. A thousand dollars."

Her eyes widened and her lips parted. Havoc couldn't tell if it was outrage or general shock at the idea. Whatever emotion she was feeling, it was negative. The other women in the room had stopped pretending to do anything other than listen to the two of them now. Spring knew it, too, because she wrapped her arms around herself as she glanced around the room.

Havoc knew Spring had to be very careful. If she indicated in any way that what he was suggesting repulsed her, she'd insult every single girl in the room. If she had another reason than some moral bullshit, she'd have to air it here or come across like a judgmental bitch. Which really should have bothered Havoc. It was a bullshit move, pure and simple.

"I-I can't," she said softly.

"Gonna have to know why. Everyone on this tier does at least one floor dance with a patron a night. We charge a pretty penny for them to have this kind of access. They get to touch, but not penetrate. They'll tip you extravagantly for the privilege on top of the grand we'll pay."

"You don't understand," she said, shivering again, wrapping her arms around herself tightly.

"Then explain it."

"I don't… like to be touched." She didn't look at him, but he could see her eyes glistening. Unshed tears? "Being naked in front of a man tends to lead to touching. Dancing definitely leads to touching."

"You managed with the stage dance well enough."

"That was different. I could control it better. Back off when I felt thr -- um, when I felt uncomfortable."

Havoc went on alert. She'd been going to say, when she felt threatened. Still, he pressed on. "Fine. Do I make you feel… uncomfortable?"

She blinked several times. "I don't know. I mean, I've never been around you." She dropped her gaze. "But it's not like you're a bunch of hands grabbing at me."

"Fine. So you'll dance three dances with me. I'll tip you, and the club pays you out a grand. Guys in the club see you out on the floor and stay thinking they'll get their turn. Club makes money. You make money. I keep you safe." He shrugged. "And comfortable."

Again, she bit her lower lip, trying to decide what to do. "I can't be completely nude. I would like my panties."

"Thong," Havoc said without hesitation.

She winced and turned her head. After what he was sure was careful consideration, she gave one sharp nod. "Fine."

He gave her five minutes to change. Before she could change her mind, Havoc snagged her hand and headed back out to the main part of the club. This would be the best money he'd ever spent in his life.

Chapter Two

Spring wasn't sure how she felt about the arrangement she'd just entered into. Fleur and her husband, Beast, had assured her everything was taken care of, that she'd be safe, but Havoc had found the one loophole they'd overlooked. And how exactly had he gotten her to agree to going out in a thong and nothing else? She'd been wearing one before, but she'd had the rest of her costume, minuscule though it had been. But a costume was like a suit of armor. In one, she was prepared for what was happening. Now, she had only the black thong, which contrasted starkly with her milky-white skin.

She'd been getting ready to leave, dressing in her street clothes. Havoc had barely given her time enough to change clothing, watching her the entire time. Had she not been wearing bikini panties instead of the thong he'd insisted, she doubted he'd have given her any reprieve at all. Spring had managed to buy herself five minutes. She'd tried for ten, but he'd said she only needed to throw on her boots and thong. Anything else would just muddy the waters.

He had grabbed her hand and headed out of the dressing room with her and now, Spring found herself on the dance floor mashed up against a wide, muscular chest. Havoc's.

Though the music was lively and drummed through her rhythmically, Havoc held her to him tightly, swaying slowly with one hand splayed wide over her back, the other sliding up and down from her hip to her shoulder. He'd insisted she wrap her arms around his neck, which was difficult because he was quite a bit taller than she was, even in her heels. Her ear was pressed against his chest where she could hear the steady beat of his heart even over the loud music.

The worst part of it -- or maybe it was the best part -- was that his scent seemed to wrap around her as much as his arms. Clean, masculine sweat mixed with a musky, woodsy smell, reminding her of the Everglades she used to roam as a child. It was probably that memory alone that kept panic at bay. When she'd told him she didn't like to be touched, she hadn't been kidding. It had been five years since she'd last had any kind of sexual touch. Up until now, she would have said she hadn't missed it. But then, Havoc wasn't really touching her sexually. Just that steady stroke of his hand along her skin. It was lulling.

There was also something about Havoc she couldn't name. A sharp forest-like kind of scent that made her nose tingle with the need to inhale even deeper. The bite of leather was present as well. He smelled like strength and comfort. Of home. And something just a little bit dangerous. The scent and feel of him, all that hard muscle and his hair-roughened arms, made her want to settle in next to him, just like she was, and stay there forever.

For the first song, he just stood there and swayed with her. His hand roaming up and down her side had a mesmerizing effect on her. Five years since she'd had this kind of human touch. A man. One attracted to her, judging by the growing bulge in his jeans.

How long had it been since she'd felt arousal and desire? Longer than that five years.

It wasn't so much because of the man, though Havoc was a prime specimen. The man was sin in a huge package. No. It was more than the man himself. It was the knowledge that he desired her. He was the one who'd put them in this situation for whatever reason. His dominance would normally have put her off. She didn't like being told what to do, or forced into situations. That's what got her in trouble the first time. But, in this case, it just seemed to fit the man. This was genuine. One thing Fleur had repeatedly told her since she'd met the woman was that the men of Salvation's Bane were very protective of women in general. While they wouldn't hesitate to punish anyone who needed it, they didn't hurt women just because they could.

Spring was taking that to heart now. If Fleur was wrong, if Spring was wrong, she was putting herself in the worst possible position.

When the second song started, Havoc flipped her around, putting her back to his chest. Spring gasped a little, pulling away slightly before he tightened an arm around her waist.

"Shh, little dancer."

Ah, God! His voice was rough and deep, right beside Spring's ear. A shiver ran through her body, and she couldn't help the little whimper of need that coursed through her with unexpected force. Hopefully, he hadn't noticed. If he did, he'd know he had her. "I want every man in the area to see how lovely you are. And that you're in *my* arms. Your little tits all perky. That beautiful little cunt might be covered with the front of that fuckin' thong, but I watched you change. It's bare and pouty. I want to know if it's getting wet. You gonna tell me?"

His hands went to her waist, sliding back and forth over the curve of her hips then back up to the sides of her breasts. He didn't cup them as she'd expected him to, but her nipples hardened as if he had. The bastard noticed, too.

"Such hard little nipples. I wonder what they taste like?"

Fuck! Why was he talking so much? She was about to melt into a puddle of goo at his feet, for fuck's sake! This had never in her life happened to her.

"Not gonna tell me if that little pussy's wet? If you don't, I'll have to check myself."

Again, she shuddered in his arms. "Y-you can't do that."

"Can't what?"

"P-penetrate me." For the first time since she'd seriously considered taking on a gig at Salvation's Angels, Spring wondered if she could do her part to enforce that rule. When Beast had mentioned before that the men could touch, but not actually penetrate her, she'd agreed. She didn't want anyone touching her in the first place. But now? If he slid his fingers inside the little triangle at the front of her thong, would she actually stop him? Because she wanted him to find out for himself if she was as wet as she knew she was.

His deep, warm chuckle at her ear said he could give two fucks about the rules. "Good thing I make the fuckin' rules then, ain't it."

"Havoc..." Her body ached for his touch. She could almost feel his fingers sliding over her bare mound to find her wet clit. What would he do if he went that far? From everything Spring had heard about the man, he pretty much did as he wanted. The only thing actually keeping her from giving him the go-ahead was that she'd heard the other girls talking and, as far as anyone knew, Havoc had never made a move on any of the girls in Salvation's Angels. He enforced the rules set forth in their contracts and had actually separated some of his men from the girls on more than one occasion. By his men, they meant the members of the MC that owned the place. Salvation's Bane. The dancers were not allowed to fraternize with the men of Salvation's Bane. Even the few club girls who worked there did not fuck the members even out of the Angels' club. Only when they were not under contract with Angels did they resume play within the club.

"Ahh. My little dancer wants my hand in her panties."

Several of the girls were on the floor with patrons. Though many of them danced nearby, several of the men dancing with them were looking straight at her and Havoc. For some strange reason, the feel of their gazes on her nearly naked body while Havoc stroked that body to madness only made her hotter.

"Please," Spring pleaded, unsure of herself and the situation. "I'm not sure... I can't..."

"Can't what? Let me get you off while all these men are watchin' us? I know you see them. I see them, too. They all have beautiful women in their arms, naked and wet, and their eyes are glued to you." He dipped his fingertips into the top of her thong, the pads brushing over her bare mound. "So fuckin' soft," he whispered next to her ear. "Move your hips, girl. Give them a show. You do a good job, I'll get you off."

Spring whimpered, doing as he said. It was crazy. She should call a stop to this immediately. Havoc was going to touch her clit. She knew he was! He was going to slide his hand farther into her panties, find her clit slick and wet, then stroke her until she came. Which would probably take all of three seconds. Instead of putting distance between them, however, she did as he asked. She rocked her hips side to side in a slow, steady movement she'd long ago perfected. Instead of being an exercise in control this time, she used it to entice. To seduce. More than one man gave up even pretending to be interested in the woman in his arms and focused entirely on Spring.

She gave herself up to the movement of her dance. And the movement of Havoc's fingers. True to his word, he slid them farther down her mound until he found her clit. Instead of stroking her like she expected, he held his fingers still. Then she realized what he was doing. The movements of her hips determined how much pressure he put on her sensitive bud, and how fast he stroked her. Once she figured that out, it was on.

Spring's hips found the rhythm of the driving music blaring all around them. Her hips snapped side to side in crisp, rapid movements. Her arms went around Havoc's neck behind her, thrusting her tits out for his other hand to find if he desired. He did. One hand gripped her breast in a firm hold, her nipple poking through his fingers. Naturally, he tightened those two fingers mercilessly, sending pleasure in a straight line from her nipple to her clit.

"Ah!" She stiffened, giving a little cry as a sudden wave of pleasure crashed over her. She was unable to keep up the rhythm with her hips, instead just doing her best to fucking stand up. When she stopped moving Havoc took over, circling her clit and drawing out the pleasure as long as he could. Unexpectedly, a second wave hit her, this one causing her to actually give a sharp scream when she came.

"My lusty little dancer," he growled in her ear. He slid the finger he'd used to touch her up to stick in his mouth. He never took his gaze from her as he sucked her juice from that thick digit. Before he pulled it completely out of his mouth, he leaned in to kiss her, his tongue sweeping inside her mouth. Instantly, their mingled flavor exploded on Spring's tongue. It was the most erotic, exotic moment of her life. Sex at its most primal. The need roiling within her was a drive she couldn't resist. In that moment, she knew she'd do whatever he wanted her to do. If that mean he intended on fucking her, she would happily go along.

"They watchin' us, girl? Watchin' me make you come?" He dipped his tongue inside her mouth again. "Watchin' my tongue fuck your mouth? Bet they're wishing they were the ones fuckin' you."

Before she could respond, he spun her around and pulled her even tighter against him. This time, his hand found her chin and he forced her to look up at him. "You see me, little dancer. No other man." That was unexpected.

"I-I see you."

His hands immediately slid from her waist to the cheeks of her ass, gripping them possessively before delivering a sharp smack to one rounded globe. "Want to let my finger trace this little thong all the way from your ass to your cunt." He did, going until it disappeared completely between her cheeks. "Want you so fuckin' wet I could slip my dick inside you with ease. I'd take you bare and fuck you 'til I came deep inside that little pussy. I'd get you so hot for me, you'd beg me for my cum." He ground himself against her, pressing her tightly to him so she felt the very impressive size of him against her belly. "You want that, Spring? You want my fuckin' cock deep inside that little pussy? You want my cum?"

How the hell was she supposed to answer that? Part of her knew it was some kind of power game he was playing. He might want to fuck, but it didn't necessarily follow that he wanted to fuck *her*. She was a convenient body he'd cornered into this for his own reasons. If she played along, would he get a kick out of how inexperienced she was? Or would she be just playing along with his game? When the next song was up, so was their agreement. They'd go their separate ways. He'd find a willing woman to fuck while she'd go home to her vibrator.

Well, after she got her son, Luca, to bed.

Havoc would definitely get the better end of that deal as far as sex was concerned. But could she actually play along with him? Did she have the courage to do it?

"Yeah," she surprised herself by answering. "I would." For emphasis, she slid her leg up his thigh to hook around his hip, opening herself up to him if he decided to take her. "Question is, how badly do you want to be inside my pussy?"

His nostrils flared, and there was a hint of surprise in those dark eyes. Instantly, his fingers dug into her hip, gripping her to him as if she'd tried to pull away and he was bound and determined to prevent it. "You're playing with fire, girl. You know that, right?"

Taking a breath, Spring decided to lay it all out there. He was the one who started this. It was time for her to finish it. "You know what the contract says. I'm pretty sure we've done too much already."

"Like hell. I can touch you as long as you don't object."

"Yeah, but you can't finger-fuck me. You can't put that big dick inside me. So you certainly can't come inside me." She gave him a sad little smile. "Pity. I'd just love to have you dripping out of me after we're both satisfied. If you fucked me good, I might even let you take my ass. Fill it just as full of cum as you did my pussy." She shrugged. "You know. Assuming you could get it up again that fast."

"Oh, I can definitely get it up a second time. Might even fill that sassy little mouth of yours the third time just 'cause I'd last longer. I could take my time. Fuck your mouth until I'm Goddamned good and ready to come."

"Sounds a little too good to be true, big guy. Anyway, it's not like it's going to happen." She grinned up at him, almost daring him to prove her wrong. What the hell was wrong with her? She couldn't do this!

Just as the thought entered her mind, the third song she'd committed to ended. With a little smirk, she pulled away from Havoc. He let her, to a point. He still kept his hold on her, but allowed her to put a little distance between them. "Aww," she tsked. "Looks like the three songs are up." She held out her hand, giving him what she hoped was a hard look. "I want my money." She tried to sound cold and experienced, so he'd think he'd had no effect on her.

Havoc narrowed his eyes, pulling her firmly back against him. "Not yet."

"Deal's a deal, Havoc. Club owes me a thousand dollars, and you owe me a tip. And it better be one hell of a tip."

For several seconds, Spring thought he might refuse. Then he nodded slowly. "Money's in my office. You'll need to come with me."

"I need to get my things first."

"Later. Come with me."

Havoc gripped her hand hard and pulled her along with him as he headed back out of the dance floor to the hallway. The stairs were just around the corner, leading to the third floor and his office. There were several rooms up there, but he took her straight to what had to be his office. Quickly unlocking it,

Havoc pulled her inside before shutting them in. He had his cell out almost before the door was shut.

"Bring Spring's things to my office, Stryker." He began the conversation without preamble. "No, just set them outside the door." Pause. "Get Glitter to fuckin' show you." He obviously didn't wait for the other man to say anything because he immediately tossed the phone onto his desk, the screen dark.

Then he pulled Spring back into his arms and kissed her again. It was hot and hungry, demanding as he slid his hand into her hair and fisted it there. She couldn't stop a little whimper, or herself from kissing him back.

Havoc didn't stop at the kiss, though. He slid his lips to her throat where he nipped and sucked until she cried out at the little sting she knew would leave a mark. Next thing she knew, he had a nipple in his mouth and his arms wrapped tightly around her.

Spring's head spun. Like she was drunk. Maybe she was. Could a person get high on sex? If so, she'd never experienced it. Not even fucking close. She ached with the need to have something inside her.

No. That wasn't entirely true. Not *something*. She needed Havoc. She'd never felt this all-consuming need in her life! Even with Luca's father, there was never a demand for her to give in to the needs of her body like this, and there had been a ton of teenage hormones involved in that experience. Along with a little too much pain at the end. Sex was pleasant at best. This… this was madness.

Just when she knew she would give Havoc whatever he demanded of her, he broke the kiss. Next thing she knew, he'd lifted her up to sit on his desk with him wedged between her legs. He gripped her ass and pulled her against him so that her pussy was mashed against the ridge of his cock. Spring just looked up at him, unable to form words or even a coherent thought beyond, *"Aren't you gonna fuck me now?"* Which she couldn't say and keep her dignity.

"Now," he said, his hand firmly on her hips. "You and I are going to have a little negotiation."

"Negotiation?" What the hell? She could hardly think, let alone negotiate.

"That's right."

"Look, my time here's up. Our agreement was for three songs. I want my money so I can get dressed."

Havoc stood there for several seconds, looking into her eyes. Spring thought he might refuse to give her what they'd agreed on, but he finally stepped away slowly. He made his way behind his desk and opened a drawer. Spring took the opening to get off the desk and snag a shirt she found draped over the back of a chair. She didn't put it on, but held it to her chest, covering her breasts. When he looked up, he sighed, a look of deep disappointment on his face before his features went blank.

He pulled out two stacks of bills. Laying one in front of her, he said, "The club owes you a grand." He nodded to the money. "You can count it if you want."

"No," she whispered. "It's fine."

"This," he raised the other bundle of bills, "Is your tip from me. Another grand."

Her eyebrows shot up. "A thousand-dollar tip? Are you out of your mind?"

He shrugged. "What you gave me was worth that and more. Which is why I have another proposition for you."

"Why do I smell a trap?"

"No trap. Just a business transaction."

"I'm not a whore, Havoc." Didn't take a genius to know where this was headed.

"Not saying you are, and I'm not trying to make you out to be one. A whore has sex for money. I want you to do it because it's what you want to do. I'm merely suggesting I pay you for your time."

"Sounds an awful lot like being a whore to me," she muttered, glad she had something to cover herself.

"I want the weekend with you," he said, ignoring her reservations. "You don't have to do anything you truly object to, but I want the chance to see how explosive we are together."

"Explosive," she snorted. "Yeah. That's a word."

He grinned. "Yeah. I'd say it was the perfect word to describe us."

"Fine. So what are you proposing?" She might as well listen to what he had to say. If it was too much, she'd simply leave.

"I want your company for the weekend."

"And?" Because that was just too simple.

"And nothing. I want your company. You spend the weekend with me. We'll see how much fun we can have." Havoc's smile was like a shark ready to take a bite out of her.

"Thought you said I wasn't a whore? Sounds like you definitely expect sex."

"Better fuckin' believe I expect sex," he said with a grin. "But you don't have to do anything you ain't comfortable with. Besides, you want sex with me. Why not do it? We're just setting a time to this relationship."

"Do everything we want to do with each other in two days." Spring turned over the thought in her mind. Not doing this wasn't acceptable. She'd learned in her short life that moments were precious. She'd given up her youth to raise Luca instead of giving the boy to her older sister, Diona, as her mother and sister had expected. The decision had cost her her family and the last of her childhood. And she'd never go back.

If she could do this without putting Luca at risk, she'd be a fool not to take Havoc up on his offer.

"I want to be able to leave if I'm uncomfortable or if it doesn't work out. I'm not going to be trapped here by an agreement."

"Good," Havoc said. "Don't want you with me unless you're havin' fun, Spring. This is an adventure. Not a punishment."

"OK then. I just need to go home and --"

"No. It's almost midnight now. I want a full forty-eight hours with you. "

"I have to make arrangements for my son. Fleur only agreed to watch him a couple of hours. That's passed a while ago."

"Wait. Your son is with Fleur and Beast?"

"Yes. Fleur said she'd put him to bed and I could stay with her tonight."

"She at the clubhouse? She and Beast have a house, but they're usually at the new clubhouse. Her and Lucy just love fuckin' decoratin'."

"She said it was a converted firehouse. She and Lucy wanted to make it more like a home for the guys." Spring wasn't sure why she felt she had to explain. Hell, it was Havoc's club. "In any case, she's at her house."

"Good. Easily taken care of. I'll let Beast know I need him and Fleur to take care of him this weekend --"

"I'm not abandoning my son so I can have a sex-filled weekend with a man I just met, Havoc. You know what? Forget it. I want to do this, but it's just not possible with no notice."

"It is, and you can. It's not like you won't see your son. We'll be in the same clubhouse, for fuck's sake! The girls bring their kids there from time to time. We ain't always havin' wild orgies, you know." He gave a shake of his head. "You wanna talk yourself out of this, you're gonna have to find a different way." He picked up his phone again. "How's the boy?" Pause. "Sleepin'? Good. Listen. I'm kidnappin' his mom. We'll be at the clubhouse most of the time, but I need you and Fleur to babysit. She mind?" Again, there was a pause. "Good. I'll tell Spring." Another pause. "None of your Goddamn business, fucker." Havoc hung up.

"Good thing you're his friend. You keep hanging up on him and he might rethink that whole relationship."

"If he's that big a pussy, I don't need him as a friend and Bane don't need him as vice president." Havoc sounded gruff, but his amused expression told another story.

"You like baiting him. Are you serious?"

Havoc laughed then, deep and rich. "Yeah, little dancer. My brothers know I'm rough around the edges. I like fuckin' with 'em to reinforce that impression." He shrugged. "Means I don't have to pretend I have manners or some shit."

Spring giggled in spite of herself. Which made her long to be with him that much more. Even if it was just for a couple of days.

"Fine," she said with a sigh. "Fine."

He raised an eyebrow. "Fine what?"

"Two days. But you're not paying me."

"I am. Keeps everything honest. We'll enjoy each other, but it's a transaction. Neither of us gets attached. Just good, clean fun."

She snorted. "Right. So, how much am I making on this little transaction?"

"I'll give you twenty-five hundred per day. That's five thousand for the entire weekend. Midnight to midnight. We'll discuss Sunday on Saturday night. If you want to call it quits then, you'll still get the twenty-five hundred."

"No questions asked?"

"Oh, I'll ask questions. Ain't sayin' I won't try to change your mind if you wanna leave."

"Hell, you might be the one to throw *me* out."

"Either way, you still get the money."

Spring thought again. Could she do this? "I don't like taking money for this."

"I'm not workin' it any other way. I don't do clingy, and I don't do permanent. If I want the girlfriend experience, I pay for it. That way there's no misunderstandings later."

"Oh, no worries on that account," she muttered. "The sex might be spectacular, but you leave a lot to be desired in making a woman feel wanted." She stuck out her hand. "It's a deal."

He took it without hesitation. "You've got fifteen minutes before midnight. You want to put on some clothes before going back to the clubhouse, your bag should be just outside the door." He pointed across the room. "Bathroom's there. Fifteen minutes and we're leavin'."

She didn't have to be told twice.

Chapter Three

The ride to the new clubhouse was longer than it needed to be. Mainly because Spring kept giggling and squealing. Apparently, the girl was having fun. Which just proved what Havoc had always known: chicks loved bikes. She kept one arm around his waist while she used her free hand to explore. Havoc had no idea if she was doing it on purpose or if it added to the pleasure she was getting from the ride, but she laid her face against his back several times while stroking his shoulder and upper arm. He'd bet his last dollar she was admiring his muscles. Which just made him smirk. Yeah. He had a lot to show this little filly.

When he pulled around to the back, several of the guys were gathered around a small fire drinking beer. As usual. Vicious threw up his hand, giving him a wave to join them. Havoc flipped him off and snagged Spring's hand. The group of men roared with laughter. Spring stiffened and resisted before letting him pull her behind him inside the clubhouse.

The patio led into the common room from the back of the remodeled firehouse, where the club girls, along with prospects and other patched members not invited to the fire outside, played pool and watched TV. Or played with a woman in the corner. More than one pair were making out. Much as Havoc wanted to try having some fun with Spring in the common room, now wasn't the time. He had to get a sense of her boundaries first. He might be paying for her time, but he would never expect her to go along with something she didn't like. He wanted her to enjoy herself as much as he did. Besides, he thought he could talk her into just about anything he wanted to try with her. He was charming like that.

The building was three stories tall. The common room used two stories of the three, and two-thirds of the length of the building -- it'd been where the fire trucks were once housed. The rest of the space on the first and second floors held the gym and old offices they hadn't yet designated a use for. The third floor held the private rooms. Some of the patched members stayed there instead of a house or other private residence. Club girls also stayed there from time to time. Havoc hadn't ever put down roots, so he had no other place. He could have, but why sink money into a house he never intended to use? The club was his family. It was all he'd ever needed. It was his room on the third floor where Havoc took Spring.

The way up wasn't uneventful. Naturally, there were several club girls hanging out. He usually took a couple-three of them in for the night when he was in the mood. Tonight, however, he wanted only Spring. Unfortunately, they didn't get inside his room unscathed.

"Hey, Havoc," Topaz called as she sidled up to him when he stopped to unlock his door. Wasn't that he didn't trust anyone in the club. He just didn't want club girls sneaking in when he didn't want them there. Topaz was friendly enough, but a bit on the territorial side, and she'd been with Havoc three of the last five nights. She draped herself over him as if Spring weren't even there. For some reason, that came close to pissing Havoc off. "I've been waiting for you to come home. Hard night at work? You know I can work out all the… kinks." She giggled at her play on words. Havoc was less than impressed.

"Not tonight, Topaz. Got company."

The other woman glanced at Spring, then dismissed her. "I'm good with an audience. Might show the little thing a trick or two."

"I said, not tonight." He let go of Spring's hand to set Topaz away from him. "Back the fuck off."

Topaz gave Spring another look, obviously reassessing the situation. "Tomorrow night then," she said, backing off but not taking no for an answer.

"I'm busy this weekend. Don't bother me." It was all he had to say. All the girls gathered around went about their business like it was nothing. Topaz shrugged, but still eyed Spring. Havoc made a mental note to keep the two women separated. Not that he planned on socializing much. He had a bounty of a beautiful woman in his room that he'd guaranteed would be there as long as he wanted. Well, as long as he didn't piss her off or scare her. Or get tired of her. All of which were entirely possible. Hell, he knew he'd enjoy the first two. He wondered if the third was even possible. Well, he had forty-eight hours to find out.

The second the door was shut, Havoc pulled Spring into his arms, kissing her wetly. She didn't resist, but didn't kiss him back with the fire she'd shown before. Her body was stiff in his arms. She clung to his shoulders, but it seemed more reflexive than a need to keep him close. It was the first time she'd been less than charmed and interested in him. Though Havoc was ready to continue where they'd left off at the club, this wasn't working.

He ended the kiss slowly, taking the time to seduce her just a little. When she relaxed somewhat, he pulled back. "Did Topaz get to you?"

"I thought this was just us. She's fully expecting to drop in."

He shrugged. "Not until Monday. Made it clear I was busy this weekend. Told you it would be just us. Ain't goin' back on that."

She glanced up at him then off to the side. "Sure." It was obvious she didn't believe him. Not that he cared. At all. "Tell you what," she said. "Maybe we should sit down and make a list."

"A list. Not following."

"You know. Hard limits."

"Sounds like a plan. Want you comfortable with this arrangement."

"Me too," she muttered, stepping farther away from him.

Havoc didn't like her putting distance between them. "We can sit on the couch. Easy to get comfortable that way."

"Fine," she said softly.

No. This wasn't going well at all.

"You know, if you're going to get clingy, I can tell you right now you're going to have to get over it." Havoc plopped down on the sofa and crossed his legs, patting the space beside him. "I told you from the outset I ain't lookin' to settle down. Just want this weekend with you because we seem to fit together well. Spark off each other." He winked at her.

"I'm not getting clingy," she snapped. "I just don't like knowing I'm going to suffer from comparison. I've been in one doomed relationship. I'm not interested in starting another one with the same type of man."

"Already told you, this ain't a relationship. It's a transaction where I compensate you for your time and we both have a lot of fun. I thought you said you could deal with that?"

"I can! Just get on with it. You got something to write this down with? Because I'm not repeating myself."

He tapped his temple. "It's all up here, baby girl. I never forget anything." Again, he patted the sofa cushion next to him.

"Right," she muttered. "Managed no man ever."

He raised an eyebrow but refrained from commenting. Funny. He'd never have thought he'd enjoy just sparring with a woman. While he didn't like Spring's obvious distress, he liked that she spoke her mind and didn't just tell him what she thought he wanted to hear. She wasn't after any of the prestige that came with his rank within the club. Maybe she really was after his money, but he doubted it. She seemed starved for physical contact. Adult interaction. A marathon weekend sex session was exactly what she needed. He could tell by the way she'd responded to him earlier.

"So," she said, sitting on the opposite end of the couch instead of next to him as he'd indicated. "I don't do ménages. Your little tarts out there can go someplace else while I'm here, and your club buddies can keep their hands to themselves. Even though I'm acting like it, I'm not a hooker. So, this is between us. I'm good with the whole one-weekend-slash-forty-eight-hours thing -- in fact, I insist on it -- but only with you."

"Agreed," he said, finding he did agree with her. Which puzzled him. Normally, he'd would have tried to get her to let him bring Topaz, or own of the other girls, in for a nice raunchy round-up, but the idea didn't appeal to him in the least. He brushed the thought aside. No need to dwell on it. "Next."

"Nothing extreme. No blood play, scat, golden showers… nothing like that. I won't do it."

"Agreed. Not sure why we're having this discussion. Sounds pretty simple to me."

Spring plowed on as if she hadn't heard him. "I'm not into age- or pet-play either. That's too dominant, and I don't know you well enough." When he opened his mouth not to agree with her, but to set her straight about the whole dominant thing -- he was a very dominant guy and would be taking charge of this little adventure -- she kept going. "Also, the first time you try to humiliate me, I'll kick you in the balls and be out of here so fast it will make your head swim. No sex in public either. What you did at the club was as far as it goes. And only because you had me at an extreme disadvantage. Not doing it again."

"I was with you until that last. No intention of humiliating you, but this is an MC. We have wild parties all the time. In fact, there's probably one tomorrow night. There's sex everywhere."

"Then when you get the urge, assuming I'm still with you by then, you can bring me back here. I'm not having sex in front of an audience. Period."

He sighed. Inside, he was rubbing his hands together with glee. That was his battle. He would talk her into this if it killed him. Not because he was a bastard, though he freely admitted he was. Because he knew she'd love it. She had responded like she was born for it at the club. She would again. "Fine. Anything else?"

"I want a safe word."

"Not a problem. Use the standard. Green, yellow, and red. You say red and we stop and talk about it. Yellow and I'll slow down. Green, we go ahead."

"Good plan. Guess you've done this a time or two."

He smirked. "You could say that. Now. Any other hard limits?"

"I want a couple of hours each day to be with my son. I don't mind introducing you to him, but I need time with him."

"Again, not a problem. I'm a son of a bitch, but I'd never keep you from your son for something like this. With Fleur looking out for him, it won't be a problem. In fact, she'll probably bring him by in the morning. The girls always do a big breakfast on Saturdays, and they bring the kids."

"Well then. I guess there's no sense beating around the bush." Spring lifted her chin. "This is your party, big guy. What's on the menu?"

It was all Havoc could do not to pounce on her. From her body language, Spring probably expected just that. She sat as far away from him as she could get on the couch with her legs crossed and her fingers laced tightly together. She wore the same shorts and T-shirt he'd made her change out of at the club before forcing her onto the dance floor with him. There should have been nothing sexy about it, but her long black hair flowing free to pool behind her where she sat and all the pale skin gleaming under the light made his fucking mouth water.

Instead of simply standing her in front of him and stripping her bare, Havoc stood and held out his hand. "Come with me."

With a sigh, she took his hand, letting him pull her to her feet. Instead of letting her hand go, however, he kept it, savoring the feel of her skin touching his. He led her out of his room and back to the common room and, more importantly, the bar.

"I thought we were here for sex," she said in a wry tone.

"We are. First, though, I thought we'd have a drink. We're both a little keyed up. Alcohol is always good to loosen things up a bit."

"I'll drink to that," she said as she leaned against the bar.

"Havoc!" Tobias greeted. "Thought you were in for the night." He winked at Spring, which had her stiffening. "What'll it be, little lady?" If Tobias knew he'd made Spring uncomfortable, he hid it well. "We have just about anything you could want as long as it's whisky or beer." He grinned.

"Jack and Coke," she said without hesitation. Or a smile. Instead, she scanned her surroundings. Havoc glanced around too. There were several patched members and some club girls, though most were out. Bane owned two strip clubs and one BDSM club, as well as two Beach Fit gyms. Likely, the guys were either at one of the strip clubs or the BDSM club. Tomorrow, there would probably be more patched members and club girls in the common room. He'd bring her tomorrow, too, so she could see for herself the club girls didn't care in the least if they got naked for the men. In fact, unless he missed his guess, Topaz was currently on her knees in the back corner with Tool, working his cock to the man's liking.

"As you wish, my lady." Yeah, Tobias thought he was charming. Havoc merely flipped him off and reached for the bottle of Jack Daniels he'd set on the bar while he got Spring's Coke and a tall glass of ice. Havoc would normally have just chugged from the bottle, but he refrained when Tobias gave him a stern look. As if that intimidated him or something. So he waited until the other man had poured a generous amount into Spring's glass before snagging the bottle and taking two long pulls.

Spring sipped her drink, eyeing him with a wary gaze. "I suppose if you get snozzled, tonight will be over before it starts. Keep it up."

"You saying you don't wanna fuck me? 'Cause I remember a wet thong that says otherwise."

Her face heated until it was beet red, the flush starting at her neck and rising. "Yeah, well, sometimes I have bad ideas. In fact, my life is full of horrible choices. So far, this is proving to be one just like all the others."

"See if you say that when the weekend's over." He nodded at her glass. "Drink up. We're gonna people-watch for a while before I take you back to my room. After that, I'm gonna fuck you until the whole clubhouse knows how good I'm makin' you feel."

Just as he'd hoped, her face and neck grew hotter, all that creamy flesh turning a deeper shade of red. With a chuckle, he moved in behind her, caging her in. She stood up straighter, taking another pull of her drink. "People-watch, huh?"

"Yeah. Like over there in the corner. That's Tool in the chair. Recognize the woman kneeling on the floor between his legs?"

"Not sure," she said softly. "It's not like I know everyone here."

"It's Topaz. Looks like she's workin' his cock good."

Tool sat with a beer bottle dangling from his fingers with one hand, while he smoothed the hair back from the woman's face with the other. She was indeed working his cock with her mouth, her head bobbing as she pumped him with one hand and let the other wander up his body under his shirt.

"Looks like he's enjoying himself." Havoc couldn't help his smirk.

"I'm not doing that," Spring said tightly.

"No one asked you to, baby. Just wantin' you to see no one here will judge you for anything you do." He pointed to another section of the common room. "Looks like they're not the only ones." Two more women had their bodies wrapped around another man, the three of them laughing and moaning, taking their pleasure unashamedly, uncaring who saw them. "Or them," he said as he pointed to another couple. "Nothing wrong with a little exhibitionism."

Spring's breathing was rapid, and her gaze locked on to the last pair he'd directed her to. "I told you I'm not into that. I won't do it no matter what you show me." But her denial was soft and distracted. Havoc grinned. He wouldn't force her into doing anything, but he'd damned sure get her to watch.

Havoc wrapped an arm around her, pulling Spring's back to his front. No way she could miss his cock pressed against her ass and lower back. "They don't mind being watched," he said next to her ear. "In fact, I happen to know for a fact more than one of 'em thrive on it."

"I don't," she said. "No matter how much you have me watch and see how much they like it, you're not getting me to do that."

His breath stirred the tendrils of hair around her ear. Havoc noted her shiver with each gentle puff of air. "Not askin' you to, baby. Just watch. See the look on her face?" He was referring to one of the club girls sitting astride one of his brothers. She was reverse cowgirl style with her hands braced behind her on his thighs. Her eyes were closed, and a little smile graced her lips, her whole face euphoric. She was fully dressed, with a short, loose skirt hiding the actual joining. She rocked atop the man while he cupped a breast. He spoke to her softly, and she giggled once, then gave a sharp indrawn breath. "See? He slid his free hand under her skirt and he's stroking her clit while she rides him. Do you think she's gonna come? I think she might."

Spring's whole body shivered. Carefully, Havoc wrapped his arms around her, and she let him have her weight. Sagging against him, she took in another ragged breath. "This is madness," she whispered.

"No, baby. It's living. Throwing your inhibitions to the wind, saying fuck it to everyone around you and just having a fuckin' good time. But you don't have to fuck in public to get the same thrill. I bet if I stroked your little pussy right now, you'd be just as wet as she is."

"Havoc..." His name was a breath on her lips, a needy plea she refused to acknowledge.

"I'm right here. Tell me what you want. I'll give you anything. Do anything to you. Hell, I want to do shit to that little body of yours that'd make you fuckin' crazy. Sit you up on the bar, spread your legs, and eat that little pussy until you scream." He poured more whisky into her glass sans the Coke and scooted it over to her. "Drink," he urged. Surprisingly, she did. Like in one big gulp with an eye-watering gasp. He couldn't prevent his chuckle. "Slow down. Just sip it."

"What are you trying to do to me?" She sounded a little resigned, but also *more* than a little turned on and curious.

"Just plying the alcohol to get you loosened back up."

"You know I'm a sure thing. Right? I mean, that's why you're paying me to be here."

"We're going to be revisiting this several times, aren't we? No, baby. I'm not paying you to fuck me. I'm paying you to just be here. I plan on getting you so horny you *want* to fuck me. Big difference."

Did she wiggle her ass against his crotch? Music was playing, though not as loud as at the club. They could carry on a normal conversation and not have to shout. Sure enough, he could feel her movements were in time to the music.

Again, Havoc poured her another couple fingers of whisky. When she brought it to her lips this time, he controlled the movement, not letting her gulp it. "Slowly, sweetheart. Just a sip."

Her body trembled in the circle of his arms again. He put one hand on her flat belly, holding her to him even as she swayed her hips from side to side in a maddening little snap. Havoc wasn't certain if she was doing it consciously or not, but her whole body seemed to move to the beat of the music.

"I think you like watching," he commented. "They certainly like you watching them. Look at Blood. He's the one fucking Mercedes underneath that little skirt she wears. She's supposed to be gone, but keeps wandering back. Part of the reason Thorn allows it is because the guys love to fuck her."

"I take it she's pretty good." Did she sound a little bitter? Her movements stopped.

Havoc shrugged. "I suppose. But she ain't got passion. Look at her. She's enjoying herself, looks like she's completely absorbed in the sensation. But you can tell the moment she starts working it too hard. Great for the guy, but I like knowin' I'm given' my woman as much pleasure as she's givin' me. Fakin' it don't do nobody no good." Just as he'd predicted, there was a subtle change in Mercedes' facial expression. There was a calculating quality there that hadn't been before. "Watch her. She's gettin' ready to get him off. Watch him grip her hips."

"Looks like she's enjoying herself enough to me."

"Watch," he said, pulling her closer and kissing the side of her neck. "Just watch."

It was Mercedes's eyes that gave her away. They narrowed as she looked back at him. She watched her partner's face intently. Blood continued to drive into her, but Havoc saw the moment Blood realized Mercedes had stopped being in the moment and concentrating on getting him off. Then she whispered something to him over her shoulder with a coy smile. Immediately, he shut down, giving one hard shove inside her then lifting him off her. He swatted her ass playfully, but tucked himself back into his jeans -- condom and all -- and stood.

"We gonna go to your room to finish?" Mercedes purred, wrapping her arms around Blood's neck. "We can talk about that property patch."

"Nope. I've got work to do." Blood looked over at Havoc and Spring and gave them a two-fingered salute, acknowledging they were watching the show. No judgment. Just letting his brother know it was all good.

Mercedes looked a little shell shocked. And livid. "But you didn't come!" Several of the club girls giggled around the room. "Shut up!"

"Sorry, honey." Blood chuckled. "I thought we were just fuckin'. Didn't realize you expected a relationship."

"You're my champion," Mercedes pouted. "You have to feel something for me if you went against Thorn and let me back in."

"Let you back in because you were fun. Now you're more concerned with being an ol' lady." He shook his head. "Ain't happenin' with me. Besides. If you were an ol' lady, you'd be dead right now."

The entire place hushed. Even several people having sex in various corners of the room stopped to listen to what was happening.

"What? I'd make you a good ol' lady, Blood. Why would you say that?"

Blood looked at her, his features hardening. "No, Mercedes. You wouldn't. Club business stays in the club. You know that."

"I've never said --"

"Only because you don't know anything important. But you've told certain people the names of every man, woman, and child in this clubhouse. If you were a patched member -- or an ol' lady -- we'd just disappear you. You're not even a club girl. You're just a rich bitch who slums around, so no harm no foul. Mostly." He took a step in her direction. Mercedes stepped back. "Leave. And don't come back. Next mess of yours I clean up will be your brains off the fuckin' floor. And you know enough to know your rich daddy can't hire enough detectives to find a fuckin' body I don't want found."

Another woman came to Blood's side, wrapping her arms around his neck and kissing him. It looked exactly like what it was. A woman diverting Blood's attention before things went to shit.

"That's Isadora. She's a club girl and works at our BDSM club as a training Domme. She's not sleeping with Blood, nor would she, but Mercedes doesn't know that."

"You had me watch all this for…? I-I thought you…"

"I am, baby. But I wanted you to see this. Not to frighten you, and I didn't think it would happen like this. He wasn't supposed to confront her yet. I thought he'd just walk away. We protect everyone in our house. Guests included. Mercedes has been leaking information she shouldn't. We were just keeping her around until we figured out who she was giving it to and why. Blood and Beast take that kind of thing personal because Beast is our enforcer. Blood's the sergeant at arms. The man we call when things go to shit and need cleaned up. Both men are in positions where, if mistakes are made and law enforcement is involved, they take the fall. Not the club. The point is, we protect our own."

He paused, but Spring kept her mouth shut.

"Anyone in this clubhouse as a guest with a club member is protected. Only women are allowed in here on their own, usually as club whores, but occasionally just to hang out. That means no one would ever humiliate you, or physically hurt you unless they saw you as a threat. You don't want to do something, you say so. I push you too hard, you go to the first patched member, prospect, or ol' lady you can find, and they'll help you." He turned her head slightly so she had to look at him. "I'm paying you to be here. At this place. With me. That's it. You want your own bed, fine. I'll try to talk you out of it, but you only agreed to be here for forty-eight hours. If I can talk you out of your panties, all the better. But it's not a requirement."

"Well, can't protest too much when I was right there with Mercedes. Or where I thought she was." She glanced up at him from under her long lashes. "I'm woman enough to admit it was kinda hot."

"Are you still? 'Cause Tool and Topaz are still goin' at it. If you need more inspiration, we can watch them for a while."

She gave him a genuine smile then, letting go a relieved breath. "No. I think I want to go back upstairs. The whisky is starting to hit, so keep it simple this first time."

He grinned. "Sometimes, simple is the best option."

Chapter Four

Spring surprised herself at how much she really wanted to have sex with Havoc. She was on him nearly before they got the door to his room closed behind them, and she wasn't stopping. She hopped into his arms, and he held her close as their lips met in a nearly desperate tango. Spring had never experienced a kiss like his before. His tongue thrust deep, and hers slid over it with a carnivorous enthusiasm. And, really, she wanted to eat him up. He was that good.

Somehow, Havoc got them to the bed, divesting Spring of her clothing as he went. He set her on her feet and jerked at her shorts until the material -- along with her panties -- pooled at her feet. He bent and picked them up, bringing the plain blue cotton bikini-cut material to his nose and inhaling deeply. His eyes closed in something like bliss before snapping open to look at her intently, growling softly.

Without warning, he snagged her around the waist and tossed her onto the bed, shoving her thighs apart roughly. "Taste," he growled. Then dove in.

In her short sexual life, Spring had never had a man do this. The father of her child hadn't cared much about her pleasure, for reasons she now saw clearly: he'd been a bastard taking his own pleasure from a woman he shouldn't have had sex with. By the time she'd figured out she could have a good time, he and Diona and her mother were long gone from her life. Thank God. She had a baby to care for and was determined to be a good mother. So, yeah. This was the first time she'd even had the opportunity to find out what she liked.

The sensations were intense and nearly too much for her to handle. She screamed and tried to push him away, but Havoc was having none of it.

"T-too much!"

"Mmmm…" He didn't stop. Shouldn't he stop?

"H-havoooooc!" She wailed his name as an orgasm washed over her, nearly painful in its intensity. "God! Oh, Gooood!" When she still tried to push him away, he grasped her hands and pinned them at her sides. Her legs were over his shoulders, unable to close unless it was around his head. He used his hold on her wrists to keep her against his mouth when she wiggled to get away, the sensation overwhelming her.

When he flicked her clit with his tongue several times, a second wave hit her. Spring had to get away from his mouth. The pleasure skirted pain just a little too much. She was hypersensitive and more than a little shocked. She came helplessly in a wet rush. Then again. Havoc was either oblivious to her distress or reveling in it. Spring had no idea. Finally, she just went limp, screaming through each wave of pleasure until sweat slickened her naked body and her voice was hoarse from her screams.

It seemed like hours before Havoc finally pulled away, wiping his mouth on the back of his hand. There was an almost maniacal gleam in his eyes as he looked at her. "Needy little thing, aren't you?"

God, that voice! It was gruff, almost a growl. Hell, the bastard *had* growled at her. But this was altogether different. This was sin and sex and dirty beyond belief. Spring might be in a state of shock, but she knew there was probably a shit-eating grin on her face right now, and she could not bring herself to give a fuck.

"Fuck, you're sweet," he continued as he crawled up the bed, opening the nightstand to snag a condom. "Gonna enjoy this just as much as I thought I would. Probably more."

"Wait!" She was just lying there! He'd just gone down on her and she was just lying on the bed, spread-eagled. Did that make her a selfish lover?

He glanced at her. "Wait?"

"I mean, yeah. Shouldn't I, you know, return the favor?"

"Don't usually turn down a blow job, but I'm not sure I'll last. Besides, we've not talked about that yet." He shook the condom packet by the edge to get her attention. "There's plenty of time. We've got all night and two more days." He ripped open the packet and rolled the condom down an impressive cock. Spring knew she should probably make him step back and give her a minute, but Goddamn, she wanted this.

As Havoc knelt below her once again, sitting back on his bent legs, he pulled her thighs over his. The position had her wide open to him. He could see everything. The way her pussy wept for him. The way her lips were swollen from his sucking. Her clit protruding proudly in her excitement. Then he aimed his cock at her entrance and tucked it between her lips.

"You ready, pretty little flower?"

For the life of her, Spring couldn't say a word. For a woman who'd been screaming to the rafters minutes earlier, now the cat had her tongue? All she could do was nod at him.

"Need the words, baby. You good? If you need a moment, we can stop."

"No!" she said, her voice husky from her cries earlier. "I'm good."

"Green light?"

"I -- yes. Yes. Green." It seemed kind of early for him to be asking her that. Early for her to be so out of sorts. "I'm sorry," she said automatically.

Havoc tilted his head at her. "Why you sorry?"

"Nothing. Just… just fuck me, already."

His chuckle warmed her already heated body. Gripping one of her thighs, Havoc fed his cock into her until the flared head was inside. "Christ, you're tight!" Spring was caught up in her own sensations, but where before he'd seemed so composed, now there was sweat beading on his forehead. "Bettin' you ain't done this since you had your son. Am I right?"

She let out a ragged breath. "Does it matter?"

Havoc rolled them over so she straddled him, his hands resting on her hips. "Nope. Just don't want to hurt you. First time, you're in control. Go as slow or as fast as you like."

Now that was surprising. Spring never expected him to be anything other than the rough, dominant man he'd already proven himself to be. Havoc wasn't mean or abusive. He just liked to be in charge. She didn't know him well, but that part was pretty clear.

She gave one experimental rise and fall of her hips, pushing herself up so her weight was braced by her hands on his chest. Wiggling a little to settle herself, Spring took time to adjust. Her pussy was stretched. While she'd managed to squeeze a baby out of it only a few years prior, she wasn't lying when she'd admitted she hadn't had sex since. No time. That made for some tight muscles, and Havoc wasn't a small man.

His hands slid up and down her thighs to her hips and back. The roughness of his palms sent shivers up her body. She liked the sensation and couldn't help but wonder how many women had felt these work-roughened hands on their bodies. Not fair, since she wasn't a virgin, but jealousy reared its ugly head, and there was no stopping the images.

The bastard grinned at her. "I think someone's out to prove something to me."

"Oh, really. And what would that be?"

"I think talking about your past sexual endeavors has made you question mine." He chuckled. "Ain't no virgin, baby. Had my share. Best thing you can do is enjoy the here and now. Don't try to compete, because it takes the fun out of it. Just like with Mercedes."

Right. And just like Mercedes, if she got clingy, Spring knew it would be a huge turn-off. She wasn't trying to screw the club over, but that was only one of Mercedes's transgressions. Mercedes obviously wanted to be with one of the patched members. Which meant she got clingy, no matter her reasoning, and that she probably wasn't picky.

"Well, no worries on that account, big guy. I'm only worried that I can't make you feel good, but I've decided I don't have to be good. I just need to be enthusiastic about it."

He outright guffawed that time. "Now you've got it."

But did she? Because she was still jealous as hell. Those club girls were probably right outside the door, waiting their turn with him. *Not tonight, bitches.*

Spring rose and fell, her body stretching better now. So she did it again, this time continuing with the movement, testing the waters. Havoc's hands gripped her hips slightly, urging her with subtle movements to keep going. Which she did. Over and over, she let her body find a comfortable rhythm and slid into it, the pleasure doing a slow build inside her. Her breathing grew more ragged both with her excitement and the exertion. Havoc seemed to take that as his cue to urge her faster.

His hands slid up her body, pulling her down on him. Spring moved her hands up his chest in mirrored action to circle around his neck as she laid her body over top of him, her hips working up and down as she fucked him. Her tits were mashed against his hair-roughened chest, making her nipples ache.

"Mmm... I think my little flower's enjoyin' the fuck outta this."

"Not saying otherwise," she purred. "Your cock feels wonderful inside me."

"Fuckin' amazing," he whispered. "Squeezin' my cock so good."

She moved faster on him, the pleasure beginning to take hold now that the discomfort had completely passed. This was another first for her. She'd never been the one on top. Hell, she'd never actually enjoyed sex much. She'd certainly never come like this. Sometimes, Christopher had taken enough time she could actually angle her body to get enough friction on her clit to come, but it had always been a chore and was never anything like the sensations Havoc was giving her now.

One thing she was discovering, being on top wasn't all it was cracked up to be. Sure, she could control the pace, but she could tell just by the feeling of Havoc's big arms as they snaked tightly around her, that she would love it even better if he took charge.

"You good now, little flower?"

"Oh, yeah," she purred, surprising herself. She was taking to this way too easily. Maybe it was the alcohol.

"Good." He rolled them over, taking time to settle himself where he wanted between her legs. His cock, still inside her, pulsed against her walls. "'Cause I'm ready to fuck the shit outta you."

"Oh…"

Then he slammed into her. Hard.

Spring let out a surprised yelp, but dug her fingers into Havoc's shoulders. He seemed to be gauging her reactions because a few seconds later, he did it again. When she arched her back, trying to get closer to him, that seemed to be his cue to do what he wanted.

Havoc pounded into her, a driving rhythm that was as ferocious as it was maddening. This was yet another first for her. Christopher had always liked to go fast with her, but he could never move like this. It was a teeth-clattering ride, and she loved every fucking second of it.

With a sharp, helpless scream, Spring came, clinging to Havoc like her life depended on it. Maybe it did. There was such a strong, all-encompassing attraction to him, Spring didn't know what to do with it. He'd repeatedly warned her not to get attached. Not to cling. But he kept giving her reasons to do just that. Was it on purpose? No. He couldn't know her desire to just have a guy want her for who she was. Not for what she could give him. She'd gone along with Diona, Christopher, and her mother because she'd thought it would make them accept her more. The second she'd found out she was pregnant -- and the little secret Christopher had hidden from her and her sister -- she'd known better.

Havoc let out a roar of his own, his cock pulsing inside her setting her off again. Her clit seemed to buzz with the effect of the overstimulation. There was no way she was going to survive this if he kept it up.

Memories of the past brought Spring down from her post-orgasmic high much sooner than she would have liked. Havoc saw it, too. He didn't frown at her, but tilted his head to the side in puzzlement.

"Love to know what thought just went through your pretty little head, flower."

"It's nothing. I've just never experienced that before." When he opened his mouth to say something, she snatched her hands away from his shoulders, pushing his chest so she could roll out from under him. She hopped off the bed and trotted through the open bathroom doorway. She cleaned herself and took care of business before going back into the bedroom once more.

Havoc casually leaned against a nearby wall, still gloriously nude. It was the first time she'd really gotten to stop and drink in his appearance. All the delicious muscles and tattoos… he was every woman's wet dream. His hair, long but shaved at the sides, was as badass as the rest of him, the long auburn strands gleaming where the moonlight shone down on him through the open window.

When she looked at him, he simply held out his hand to her. Without a word, Spring took it. She expected him to kiss her, or start feeling her up again, primed for more sex, but instead he pulled her into his arms and rested his chin on the top of her head.

"Did I hurt you, Spring?"

"No," she said, startled by the question. "Not at all."

He squeezed her once before scooping her naked body into his arms and going to the bed. He lay down with her, spooning her against him. All that muscle wrapped around her in a protective cocoon. Yet one other thing about him that made her want to cling. Which she absolutely could not do.

"Rest, baby. Tomorrow morning, we'll have breakfast with your kid. Then we're goin' on a ride."

"Ride? Where?"

His warm chuckle thrilled her. They'd just had sex, and here she was wanting him again. "You'll see. Gonna have some fun with you tomorrow."

"If you think you're taking me back to the club, you can think again. I'm not having sex with you in public."

He gently grasped her chin and turned her head so she could see him as he leaned up and over her. "Honey, you told me that was a hard no. I confess I considered trying to talk you into it, but we've only got two days and I'd much rather spend that time takin' you any way and every way I can that you're not opposed to. After that, we might re-evaluate the situation."

"If you mean you paying me to stay longer with you, forget it. Two days, Havoc." She couldn't help herself, yawning on the last. It was probably close to dawn, and she was exhausted.

"We'll see, baby. Now, sleep. You're wilting."

"Can't deny that. But don't think you've worn me out. I've been awake all day preparing for my performance at the club. The down from the adrenaline rush was more than I expected."

Again, he chuckled. "You keep tellin' yourself that, kid. I was here for your screams. Which, I might add, were fuckin' constant."

"Whatever." Snuggled into his warmth, she noted he had his arms tightly around her, then she was asleep.

Chapter Five

"Good morning, sir. I'm Luca."

Havoc wasn't sure what he'd expected when he'd set up breakfast for Spring with her son, but the precocious little boy with glasses too big for his face and a somber expression wasn't it. The kid held out his hand, looking as if he fully expected Havoc to take it. Slowly, he extended his own hand and grasped the boy's, careful not to squeeze too tightly.

"I'm Havoc," he said, introducing himself.

The kid's face screwed up. "Like in the comic book?" Havoc shrugged. "He died in the movie, you know. Not sure you'd be more better than him 'cause he had superpowers." With that, the kid hopped up on a chair and helped himself to the syrup for the massive pile of pancakes on his plate. Beast snickered while Fleur tried her best to hide her grin by giving a delicate cough.

It wasn't long before Spring entered the room. She'd dressed in blue jeans that molded her curves deliciously and a T-shirt she tied at the waist. Little white canvas shoes were on her feet with no socks.

"Hi, Mommy," Luca said before shoving a huge mouthful in his mouth. "'Is welly go', ao'ey!"

Spring smiled... and the whole fucking world lit up. How could a woman be so... beguiling? It was hard to reconcile the woman squirming in his arms last night with the sweet, innocent little thing smiling down at her son now.

"I'm glad the pancakes are good, sweetheart. But don't talk with your mouth full, OK? Chew, swallow, then thank Fleur for the pancakes." The reprimand was gentle, and the boy grinned around his mouthful. Then swallowed all that was left in a huge gulp.

"Thanks, Fleur. I'm glad you didn't let Beast cook. I bet he's a horrible cook."

Beast growled at the boy who only giggled. Apparently, he'd been doing that a lot around the kid. "I can cook."

Fleur mouthed, "No he can't," shaking her head with a superior expression on her face. Luca giggled before scooping another enormous bite into his mouth.

"Looks like you guys are gettin' along great," Havoc said, hoping to help put Spring at ease. "He's even got Beast pegged pretty good."

"Are you sure you don't mind watching him a little longer? I hate to be a bother, Fleur."

"Pfft! No bother. He's a charmer, that one. Doesn't take it easy on the fragile male ego, either. I like him."

Syrup dripped from Luca's chin as he grinned around yet another mouthful.

"He can stay with us as long as you need him to."

Spring sighed, fixing her own plate, albeit with a far smaller portion. Honestly, how the kid was eating so much was beyond Havoc. As he watched in fascination, Luca kept shoveling pancakes and syrup into his mouth, showing no signs of slowing down. Beast glanced at Luca's plate, then at the dwindling stack of food. Havoc realized at the same time there wasn't going to be much left. Both men dove for the plate, prompting a startled laugh from Luca, who promptly expelled the food in his mouth everywhere in his mirth. Though Havoc managed to procure two pancakes for himself, Beast got the drop on him, snagging four.

"Bastard," Havoc muttered. At which Luca giggled. Havoc kept the same angry expression on his face he'd addressed Beast with but turned to the boy and winked. Luca tried to wink back, but only succeeded in blinking.

"I just hate to put you out, Fleur," Spring continued. "It's not as if it's an emergency now."

Fleur raised an eyebrow. "You sure about that? Did you get all you needed at the club last night?"

"Close enough," Spring said softly, looking down at her plate. Her hand trembled and for some reason, Havoc couldn't stand the sight. He reached over and gripped the hand holding her fork and squeezed. When she looked up at him in surprise, he held her gaze.

"Looks like we have something to discuss."

She shook his hand off before replying, "No. We don't." She turned her attention to Luca, who was sitting there looking at the adults with a worried expression on his face. He'd finally stopped eating. "Baby, go wash up. Do you know where the bathroom is?"

"I'll take him," Fleur said. "Gideon, would you mind getting Luca's dishes? He was wanting you to take him on a lap around the compound on your bike if it's OK with Spring." Gideon was Beast's real name. Only Fleur ever called him that, and only when something was important. At least, as far as Havoc could determine.

To her credit, Spring just smiled. Luca gave her a pleading look. "Please, Mommy?"

"If you promise to do everything Beast tells you."

"I promise! I promise!"

"Then go. Wash. You'll get sticky syrup all over his bike, and then you'd have to help him wash it."

Beast just chuckled. "Better hurry, kid. Bike leaves in ten minutes."

"Oh, boy!" Luca jumped down and ran full speed into the bathroom, Fleur right behind him.

"See? He's fine. Fleur and Beast have a full day planned, I'm sure."

"Looks that way." She sighed. "Where are we going?"

"I told you it's a surprise." He stood and snagged her hand. "Come on."

"I have to clean up the dishes! Havoc, stop!"

"Beast can do it," he said, looking back over his shoulder. Beast flipped him off but snagged both their plates and put them in the dishwasher.

"Gonna use the beach today. That good?"

Beast shrugged and nodded. "I'll make a note. You can have it the rest of the day if you want."

"Thanks," he said before snagging Spring's hand and taking off.

"Where is everybody?" Spring asked as they stepped outside. "I figured the place would have at least some people here on a Saturday."

"Normally, but most everyone went on a ride. Not planned or anything. One goes, they all go." Havoc wasn't remotely interested in the others in his club right now. He wanted to get Spring off to himself. If they needed him, they knew how to find him.

Once she was securely on the back of his bike, he took off. The sun was warm and the air coming off the ocean cool as they sped down the road. Havoc loved the feeling and, judging by the giggles behind him, Spring did, too.

The spot he drove them to was a little, out-of-the-way cove on an old property the club owned. ExFil, the paramilitary organization owned by the Bones president, Cain, used the beach to train and to practice beach maneuvers. It was closed to the public. As it happened, the place was totally empty today.

Havoc smirked. He might not get Spring to let loose her need for exhibitionism, but he could get her to pretend. This was the absolute perfect spot for that.

The beach wasn't large, but it was secluded, and they kept the sand clean and free of litter. The cove was well off the road and at the base of a cliff. They were literally surrounded on all sides by either water or the cliffside. The club had made a small parking lot halfway down the slope on a wide shelf of rock they'd extended which provided shade and easy access to the property, blocked by security fencing with keycard and PIN access only, not to mention security cameras at all different angles. Havoc parked his bike then snagged a backpack he'd lashed to the back of his bike and led Spring down the stairs to the pristine white sand beach.

"I wish you'd said something. I'd have had Fleur bring me a swimsuit."

"Don't need one," he said with a grin. "I have it on good authority that this is a nude beach. No swimsuits allowed."

"Havoc…" She sighed.

He silenced her with a kiss. "Not to worry, my shy little flower. Cain owns the property, and it's closed. You saw the security. No one gets in without us letting them in." Just as he'd hoped, she eyed the water longingly, considering what he'd said. Havoc saw the exact moment she decided to give in to temptation.

A huge grin spread across her face. "Race you to the water." Then she took off, leaving a trail of clothing in her wake.

* * *

Never in her life had Spring even considered skinny dipping. Now, she hopped from one foot to the other to kick her panties aside, then plunged headlong into the warm waters of the Atlantic off Florida's east coast. The sun felt wonderful on her bare body, adding to the eroticism of the moment. This was just another reason she was glad she'd taken Havoc up on his offer to pay her to spend the weekend with him. Yet another first she'd ticked off on a list that was growing rapidly by the hour.

She ducked under a wave only to have a strong arm snake around her waist. When she emerged from the water, she cried out only to burst into laughter when Havoc dug his fingers into her side to tickle her ribs.

"You cheated, you little brat!"

"All's fair and love and war, you ape!"

"Yeah? Which one does this fall under?"

Spring snorted. "War, of course. Love is for pussies."

Havoc roared with laughter. Even with the full beard, when the man smiled, it had a devastating effect. This genuine laughter was even worse on her poor senses. He was dangerous. Not because of his physical strength or because he was vice president of an obviously well-connected and probably dangerous MC. Havoc could break her heart faster than she could say *scat* and never break a sweat doing it.

He wrapped his arms around her, their bodies gliding together sensuously. "Knew I could get you naked in public."

"Well, unless you're lying, this isn't public. You said it was a private beach."

"It is. But you're still out in the open. Skinny dipping. Sun warming your skin. Little nipples all puckered just waitin' for me to suck on 'em."

Her breath caught. God, the man was wicked! "I suppose I am. Does this mean you're gonna fuck me here?"

"Now you're gettin' it," he said with a grin. She felt his cock mashed between them, pulsing occasionally against her belly. "Put me inside you," he said.

Spring didn't hesitate. Her fist barely fit around his length as she wrapped her fingers around him, stroking a couple of times just for the experience. The skin was soft, but the core was steel. As she guided him into her, all Spring could think of was the exquisite stretch and the intense sensations it brought on.

Havoc held her gaze as he filled her. The water rolled around them gently in frothy waves. Spring completely lost herself in the moment and the man. Muscles flexed and rippled as he worked her body. Gulls called off in the distance, a witness to what they were doing.

When she reached the point where she needed more, she tightened her legs around him, and used her heels to dig into his ass. Moving her body faster, she reached for her orgasm. It was there, just out of reach.

"Havoc," she whimpered. "I can't…"

"I've got you, baby," he said, bringing his hand between them. His thumb found her clit, and it set her off. She screamed, writhing on him as she came in a wet rush. Her pussy clenched around him, too small to comfortably clamp down. Which was its own pleasure. Havoc gave a startled shout and swelled impossibly bigger when she came. Had he felt that big the last time? The burn she experienced now was beyond exquisite. The slight pain morphed into the most intense pleasure. The second wave hit her hard, so hard she thrashed and bucked in reaction.

"Fuck! Fuck!" Havoc bit out, gripping her hips. It almost seemed like he was trying to push her away. But that couldn't be right. Could it? "Baby, you gotta let up. Let me go."

"Havoc!" She cried his name, clutching him closer. Let him go? Was he serious? She couldn't let him go. She needed him to keep giving her this. To hold her tighter. "Please," she whimpered. "Don't leave. Don't leave."

"Ah, fuck, baby." Then he threw back his head and roared, clutching her as tightly as she did him. His arms were so tight around her she could barely breathe, but Spring loved it.

For long moments they stood there. Havoc nuzzled her neck, kissing her and sucking the delicate skin there. A deep, satisfied rumble from Havoc reverberated through her body. "Yeah," he said, rubbing her back. "I gotcha, baby. I gotcha."

Finally, after she caught her breath, Spring lifted her head from his shoulder to look into his supremely satisfied face. "That was…"

"Yeah. It was. You good?" There was an odd look on his face she couldn't interpret.

"Yes. It was wonderful." Unexpectedly, a blush stole up her face. "I've never done that before."

"Done what?" His gaze narrowed.

"Sex in the ocean." She giggled. "Or water of any kind. And being out in the open didn't bother me at all. Mainly because I couldn't concentrate on anything. The sun and the sea… it was all like another hand stroking me. I'm still not letting you fuck me in front of anyone, but I can see how a person could lose themselves so completely it wouldn't matter."

He grinned at her. "Yeah. I noticed you were lost in the moment."

That didn't sound good. "Did I do something wrong?" Her chest tightened at the thought. Racking her brain, she tried to think of anything she'd done to anger him or if, God forbid, she'd hurt him. But that was ludicrous. He was much bigger and stronger than she was. If she did something that hurt, surely he'd have just repositioned her.

When she stared up at him helplessly for several seconds, Havoc kissed her once softly on the lips. Then asked a question she'd never expected.

"Baby, are you on the pill?"

"I -- no. I never had the need to…" She trailed off as the reason for his question finally sank in. "Oh, God…"

He sighed, pulling her close once more. Neither of them spoke, just holding each other. It felt odd to Spring. They both had been so flippant about how this was a weekend fling. How could she have forgotten? Because it was her. He'd tried to push her away, had tried to be the responsible one. Spring had been the one so lost in her own pleasure she'd locked her legs around him and refused to let him pull out of her.

"I'm so sorry," she whispered. "This was all my fault."

"Honey, I'm the one who started it. I thought I had enough control not to come in you. Don't tell my brothers, by the way. I'll never live it down."

That little bit of humor on his part didn't help her anxiety. "How can you laugh at this?"

"I'm not, baby. I was trying to make you feel better."

She took a deep breath and let it out slowly, trying to center herself. Funny. She remembered doing that the first time she'd ever had sex. It had been with Luca's father. She'd taken that same deep breath in and let it out slowly before sex then. Now, after a vastly different experience, she did the very same thing. Unlike the first time, this breath didn't calm her nerves.

"I can tell you I'm clean," Havoc offered. "And I've never had sex bareback. Wanted to feel your tight little pussy around me just once without anything between us. It was a selfish move. I admit it."

"I've not had sex since Luca was born." She figured she might as well lay everything out for him. Because, fuck if she knew what to do now. "My doctor did a bunch of tests when I first found out I was pregnant, and I was clean. I've not been tested since, but there's not been any need. Can we go back to the beach? Out of the water and the sun?"

"Sure, baby. Under the parking lot we've set up a break area for the guys to get out of the sun and the elements. We can relax there for a while."

Surprisingly, Havoc took her hand and led the way out of the water. His thumb brushed over the back of her hand several times. When they reached the covered area he'd indicated, he reached into the backpack he'd brought with him and tossed her a towel before getting one for himself.

It was several minutes before he turned back to her. His expression was unreadable, but he didn't look unapproachable. Spring wrapped the towel around herself and sat on one of the lounge chairs. Havoc sat as close to her as he could, his own towel wrapped around his waist.

"I can't take a morning-after pill, Havoc." She thought it was best to get to the point. He sat up straighter and she thought, "Here it comes," meaning the explosion of indignation about why couldn't she take it? If she was so morally opposed to it, why was she out fucking any Tom, Dick, or Harry who paid her? Her shoulders hunched in anticipation.

"Girl, what makes you think I'd want you to do that? It's your body. If you're pregnant, you are the one who has to decide what to do. I'm not so big a bastard that I'd leave you to it." He sighed and reached for her hand. "I don't lie, Spring. I'm the vice president for Salvation's Bane. To do my job effectively, I have to know I can trust those close to me and the club. I don't lie to them. I expect them not to lie to me. So, I want you to really hear me. I'm not going to pretend to love you. I'm not going to pretend we're in an exclusive relationship. What I will do is promise to help you any way I can with whatever you need from me." He reached forward and lifted her chin so she had to tilt her head to look at him. "Understand me?"

It was really simple. He didn't love her. She didn't love him. She *liked* him. A lot. But they didn't know each other, and she was still having difficulty with the fact he'd paid her to stay with him that weekend.

"You know," she said, deciding it was best to just lay everything out. "If I didn't need the money, there's no way I'd be here right now." Havoc didn't say anything. She was probably insulting him, but she had to get this out. "But, now that I am…" She looked up at him, suddenly overcome with emotion she had been holding back for a very long time. "I'm really glad. I never thought I could have this much fun with sex." She sniffled and gave a little giggle. "And, so far, it's been really fun."

He smiled at her. "I told you we needed to have a talk. Guess this is it. I want to know why you need money this badly."

"You know, that has nothing to do with what's happening to us now."

"No, but, like you said, it got you here."

"Luca… is my brother-in-law's child."

Chapter Six

Havoc wasn't sure where she was going with this, but he was willing to hear her out. Spring was many things, a brat among them, but he didn't think she was a liar. She was dead wrong to think this little SNAFU was her responsibility. If it was anyone's fault, it was his.

It had been his arrogance in believing he could control himself if he dipped bareback inside her. Just for a few seconds, or so he'd planned. He'd known she was tight, but hadn't been prepared for the feel of it. He'd never done it without a rubber before because of this very thing. He didn't want kids.

Or rather, he hadn't. Still wasn't sure, but he was disturbed by the relief that flooded him when she'd told him she couldn't take a morning-after pill. She hadn't mentioned abortion, but he got the feeling that wasn't an option for her either. He also got the feeling he was about to find out why she couldn't take the pill. And it wasn't some moral issue with her but a medical one. He felt that in his soul.

"Why were you screwing your brother-in-law?" That didn't seem like her either.

"It wasn't exactly by choice. I thought I had to."

"Christ," he swore. "How old were you?"

"Sixteen. Not old enough to actually consent, but Christopher said not to worry. He'd take care of it."

When she didn't continue, he prompted her. "I suppose there's a reason for this?"

"My sister couldn't have children. She and my mother decided I would surrogate. When they told me about it, I wanted to wait until I'd finished high school and college, but my sister wanted to try right away. She said her husband, Christopher, wasn't getting any younger and was worried he couldn't be an active father if they waited another six or seven years for me to finish school. My sister is ten years older than me, and her husband is seven years older than her."

"Fuck, he's younger than me. And that was five years ago?"

"Yeah. But that's just the excuse Diona and my mother gave me."

"I take it there was more than age going on with Christopher's objection to you waiting to surrogate?"

"You could say that. He's a corporate attorney. Rakes in the big bucks. He got one of his golfing buddies to be my OB when I went to get checked out to make sure I was healthy enough to do this. He basically looked at my lady parts and pronounced me ready for baby-making. Christopher went with me and explained the whole surrogate thing to the doc, like they hadn't already discussed this before, and he proceeded to lay out our options. I could go through in vitro, or do it the good old-fashioned way. Since Christopher was married, and I was not having sex with my sister's husband, the doc handed Christopher a pamphlet on the services he offered in the office, and we left."

"Great. What next?"

"He and Diona discussed it. They decided it was too expensive to do the in vitro on his limited budget." She scoffed. "Man had money for the latest sports cars for both him and Diona. I never understood why he didn't have money for this. I mean, it was supposed to be his child. Right?"

"I think I see where this is going. He talked his wife, who was already seven years younger than him, into letting him sleep with her sixteen-year-old sister. To make a baby for him and his wife to raise."

"Pretty much."

"Why do I have a feeling there's more?"

She sighed. "Because there is. It took six months of 'trying' before I got pregnant. Christopher was monitoring my periods, but not that closely. His solution was to wait a week after my period, have sex with me every night for two weeks, then repeat the cycle until I got pregnant."

"Sounds like he had more on his mind than just making a baby."

"Yeah. He never asked me to take a test or anything. He'd just show up a week after my period ended to have sex with me every night. I was stupid for allowing it, but I did it for Diona."

"Why? Why put your future on hold when she was disregarding your happiness?" The more he heard, the more Havoc started to ache inside. He supposed his first instinct should be to discount this because her tale was kind of out in left field. Who did this kind of shit? And why would any self-respecting woman allow her man to screw her sister with the sole purpose of putting a baby inside her? And Spring had only been sixteen. Though Havoc had seen worse, this was just crazy. But he believed her. Every single word.

"Because it's what she and my mother wanted."

"Not a reason, baby. It's your body."

"Havoc, I was what you might call a change-of-life baby. My mother never planned on having more than one child. She and my dad got set in their careers before they started trying. When they conceived Diona, my mother was thirty-nine and my father was forty-two. One child was all they'd planned for. I think my mother lived her life through Diona. My sister got whatever she wanted. Then I came along and ruined everyone's carefully laid plans. I never felt like I was wanted by anyone other than my dad. He doted on me, which made Diona hate me that much more."

"Where's he?"

"He died when I was seven. Heart attack. If he'd been alive, this would never have happened."

"So, you agreed to this because you thought they'd... what? Accept you?"

"Love me," she said softly.

That just about broke Havoc's heart right there. He rubbed his chest absently, actually feeling the pain. "Baby, that's not love. That's manipulation."

Spring snorted. "Says the biker who's paying me to stay with him for the weekend."

"I didn't manipulate you into this, but I know you were making a point. Look, I know enough to know that love doesn't make you do anything you're uncomfortable with. It especially doesn't ask you to fuck your sister's husband."

"Well, it gets worse. When I suspected I might be pregnant, I went to my family doctor. She did blood work and a urine test. There were some things she didn't like. Like my blood pressure was through the roof, I was getting migraines, and I had zero energy. Sometimes, I'd get so short of breath doing everyday activities -- like cleaning the house -- I had to stop and sit down. During the exam and subsequent testing, she found two issues. First, I had a hole in my heart. Probably had it since I was born. It wasn't too bad, but it had reached a stage where it needed immediate repair. I'd mentioned I was also bleeding excessively with my periods the last couple of months, but that my current one was a few days late. To be safe, she did a pelvic exam. When she did, she asked if I'd had the IUD placed to help with the heavy periods."

"Wait. Why didn't you tell the first doc you had the IUD? That would definitely complicate getting pregnant."

"Because, I didn't have one. At least, I didn't know I had one. She got my records from the OB office and, sure enough, the day I was examined to make sure I was healthy enough to conceive, the doc had actually put in an IUD instead. According to what he recorded, I was there for irregular and heavy periods. Not the first or best way to treat that, but certainly an option when other forms of management aren't feasible."

"So the bastard just wanted to fuck you. And he got his wife's permission to do it."

"That was my assumption. Anyway, she removed it, and I got the news that it had failed. I was pregnant. Yay." She gave a false cheerful fist pump. "Look," she said. "I told you all this to explain why I can't take the morning-after pill. I had to have heart surgery pretty quickly after that. I debated on what to do. The specialist I saw said the baby could and possibly would be harmed if they put me under to do the surgery, but if I didn't get my heart fixed, no way would I survive the pregnancy."

"Reasonable to think you'd choose the surgery."

"Not right away," she said slowly. "Even though he'd lied to me and probably my sister and my mother, I felt I owed it to all of them to let them know what was going on. My sister was livid."

"I imagine so. Though, I can't feel sorry for her. She gave him the green light. He just took it further than she intended."

Spring gave a humorless laugh. "That would be the assumption, wouldn't it? She'd be mad at Christopher for putting me on birth control before trying to have a baby with me so he could have a young piece of ass any time he wanted. But no. My dear sister said it was just like me to manufacture a reason to get rid of her baby right when she was about to 'have a child and be happy.' Her words. My mother felt nearly the same way. Which is when I left. I was still on my mother's insurance, and she couldn't do anything about it until the next open enrollment, so I had the surgery. Fortunately, Luca survived. The surgery had no ill effects on the pregnancy." There was her soft smile. There was no doubt in his mind she loved that little boy. The small interaction he'd had with them this morning left no doubt in his mind.

"Did you stay?"

"At home? Hell, no! Not only did they make me feel like shit when I told them I had to have the surgery, but, when Luca continued to grow with no noticeable problems, they started putting pressure on me to continue with our arrangement and give Luca to Diona and Christopher."

"Where are they all now?"

"Far as I know, Christopher still works for the same law firm here in Palm Beach, and he and Diona still live in their estate. Mom lives in the same condo."

"So you don't see them."

"Only on court dates. Christopher is still trying to get custody. I got a reasonable judge, believe it or not. Given the strange nature of conception and the fact that I was only sixteen at the time, the judge gave me full custody. She was inclined to believe my story, probably because of my age, though Christopher claimed I was a manipulative teenager and tricked him into it. Just so happens I got caught. I'm pretty sure it was touch and go at the time as to whether or not they were going to bring him up on charges for having sex with a minor. I'm sure his money smoothed the way for him." She looked up at him, meeting his gaze then skittering away. "Do you believe me?" Then she said quickly. "I swear I'm not lying."

"Little flower girl, I've been the vice president for this MC for nearly ten years. Part of it for more than twenty. You don't get my job without learning when you're being lied to. You ain't lyin'."

"Thank you," she said softly, a tear dropping from her eye before she could blink it back. She dashed it away with the back of her hand. "So, the reason I can't take the morning-after pill is the hormones. I had surgery to fix my heart, but I have to avoid anything that could mess with it. The hormones in birth control mess with me something horrible. Caffeine and alcohol are concerns, too, but as long as I don't drink either heavily, my doctor doesn't have too big a fit."

"Which stops now."

"Huh?"

"The caffeine and alcohol. And anything else she suggests. You on any medications? What if you are pregnant? Will the hormones harm you?"

"Just a multivitamin to keep my iron up. I've had problems with it since my pregnancy. And she said if I do want to have more kids in the future it would put me in the high-risk category, but it was certainly manageable with the right doctor and treatment. She even told me to let her know if the situation arose, and she'd get me any referrals I needed."

"Good. From now on, I'll make sure you stay on top of this. You'll also make an appointment with her and discuss this. If you're not pregnant now, you should still keep current with her."

"Why are you doing this? After this weekend, I'm gone. The reason I needed the money was for lawyer fees. Christopher is making it hard on purpose, knowing he can outlast me in the money department. What I've already got catches me up. This weekend pays for a few more hours. Hopefully, that will settle it. If not, I'll have to work it out in a different way, because if Christopher catches me working at a strip joint, I'll lose Luca for sure. To say nothing of this. Your girls in the club get wind of our arrangement, he'll find out. Shit like that doesn't stay hidden. It always finds its way back to someone who can use it against you."

"Doin' this 'cause I fuckin' feel like it, OK?" That came out harsh, but he must have looked uncomfortable enough she took pity on him. She smiled again, and his heart just fucking melted.

"Fine. But don't think this gives you license to run over me when you feel like it. I've been on my own since I was sixteen. I'm not going to just lay down and take it."

Havoc couldn't help himself. The grin on his face probably looked predatory, but he was feeling that way at the moment. "No. I expect you'll ride me as hard as I ride you."

"Havoc! That's not what I meant. Not even close!" But she laughed again. And that was good enough for Havoc.

* * *

After their talk, Havoc had taken Spring two more times. He'd used a condom because he knew she'd be more comfortable, but since he'd had a taste of her, he'd developed this predatory, possessive frame of mind that didn't seem to want to go away. It was why he fucked her after she'd bared her soul to him. He didn't want her to regret telling him or to think he was done with her. In fact, he was seriously rethinking their arrangement. He wasn't certain the weekend was going to be enough.

Something about Spring, or maybe just knowing her predicament, had triggered something inside Havoc that was so uncomfortable it became a physical ache. He had the urge both to push her away and to keep her close. He wanted to lose that pain inside him before it took root, but suspected it had already set fast. The only way to fix himself was to help Spring, then to keep her close. He tried to slam the door on that thought, but when he tried, the ache only increased.

It was early evening, the sun just starting to set, when he pulled into the Salvation's Bane compound with Spring on the back of his bike. Again, he'd taken the long way home because she'd enjoyed the ride so much. God help him, he was in so much trouble.

She placed a hand on his shoulder as she dismounted, and he reached out a hand to steady her. She gave him an appreciative smile, and he squeezed her shoulder once before getting off the bike himself. He snagged her hand as they walked toward the back of the clubhouse where they could hear a child's carefree cries.

"Mommy!" Luca bounded from the backyard at full speed toward Spring. She slipped her hand from Havoc's and reached out her arms for the little boy. Havoc could see a disaster looming. The child was small, but so was Spring. Sure enough, when he flung himself at her, into her arms, Spring stumbled backward and would have fallen, but Havoc caught both mother and child.

"Careful there, munchkin," he said to Luca as he scooped both of them up into his arms and carried them to the back of the house. "You'd've both ended up on your ass if I hadn't come along."

Luca giggled. "Wow! You're pretty strong!"

"That's right," he growled, winking at the boy. "Don't you forget it, either. Strong enough to whip your little butt, kiddo."

"You can't spank me. Mommy'll spank *you*."

He snorted. "I'll whip your mom's butt even harder."

"Havoc!" Spring scolded, ruining the effect by giggling.

Immediately, Luca stilled, giving Havoc a fierce glare. The kid looked almost feral in that moment, and Havoc knew he'd fucked up.

"You hurt my mommy, and I'll hurt you worse," he said. They'd reached the back yard, and Havoc let the pair down. Spring looked bewildered, obviously seeing the change in her son. The second he was free, Luca kicked Havoc in the shin. Hard. Havoc grunted, but otherwise didn't go after the kid. He was going to address it, but not right that second. Luca needed to calm down first. He was only four, so this had to be handled carefully.

The kid ran several feet away before turning around and baring his teeth at Havoc. At once, Spring went to the child. "Luca!" She reached him and tried to pull Luca into her arms, but he squirmed, never taking his eyes from Havoc. What surprised Havoc the most was how Luca kept himself between Spring and Havoc. It was almost as if Luca knew Spring would follow him if he ran. Having gotten his mother away from the man he now saw as a threat, he seemed determined to keep her safe himself.

Beast stood off to the side, gripping Fleur's shoulders when she'd have stepped in, likely to reassure the boy Havoc would never hurt them. Luca wasn't panicked at all. He just kept his gaze steady on

Havoc, baring his teeth every now and then. Spring tried to gain his focus, but Luca was having none of it. His little hand rested on his mother's shoulder, but he didn't give her his attention.

Slowly, Havoc approached the pair, hands open and out to his sides slightly, trying to put the boy at ease. He sank down in front of the child before speaking. "Luca, I'd never hurt you or your mother."

"You said you'd spank her. Spankin's hurt."

"True. They do. Has your mom ever spanked you?"

Luca gave him a wary look, like he sensed a trap but didn't know how to get around it. "Yeah. But I'm a big boy. I can take it."

"Did it mean she didn't love you? Or that she wanted to really, really hurt you?"

"N-no. She hugged me after and cried with me."

"Spankin's ain't meant to harm. They're meant to correct bad behavior. I might spank your mom if she put herself or you in danger, but I'd never hurt her. Mostly, I'd spank her to tease her because your mother would never, ever put you in danger. And I'd hold her after, just like she did you. I'd never hurt her like you're meanin', Luca. I'll protect you both from anyone who would hurt you. Do you understand the difference?"

The little boy took his time thinking, studying what Havoc had said. He didn't once look at Spring, making up his own mind. "I think so. Like, if Mom let that man at the courthouse take me away, you'd spank her?"

Everything in Havoc stilled. Spring took in a sharp breath, and Havoc placed his hand on her arm to keep her quiet. "What man, Luca?"

The kid shrugged, finally glancing at his mother. "He was talking to Mommy. I heard him say he was taking me with him whether she wanted him to or not." For the first time, the child looked scared. "You won't let him, will you, Havoc?"

Spring collapsed in a heap on the grass, pulling Luca with her. She wrapped her arms around the child and sobbed into his neck. "I'm so sorry, baby. I swear, I'll never let you go. Never."

"No one's gonna take you away from your mother, Luca. Ain't gonna let that happen, no matter what."

Luca looked up at him then, his eyes gleaming with intelligence and an awareness no child of four should have. "He said he'd hurt Mommy, Havoc. Said he'd get me one way or the other."

Havoc turned his gaze to Spring. "He say that to you?"

"I-I didn't think Luca heard," she said.

"So he threatened you."

"Yes," she whispered.

Yeah. Havoc was in a world of trouble. Because he was fixing to find this Christopher motherfucker and fuck him the fuck up. He tried to tell himself it was because Spring was a good person and a good mother and didn't deserve that kind of harassment. He tried. But the thoughts of her out in the world without him there to protect her and Luca just wouldn't materialize. When he thought of the two, he thought of them here at the clubhouse. Or, better yet, in his home. Which was crazy because, again, he'd known them both less than twenty-four hours. Besides. He didn't fucking have a home other than the clubhouse.

Fuck. This wasn't good.

"Don't worry, Luca," he said. "No one's gonna hurt you or your mom. No one's gonna take you away from her. And you guys are never gonna be on your own again."

Chapter Seven

The rest of the afternoon was spent in the clubhouse backyard. Several members of the club introduced themselves. This was a side of Salvation's Bane she hadn't expected. Yes, they were preparing for a party that night that promised to be even wilder than the one the night before. But they were cordial to Spring, and showered Luca with enough masculine attention to make the child relax once again.

When he'd confided in Havoc his fear Christopher would take him away from her, it had broken Spring's heart.

As to Havoc's declaration to protect them, she didn't put much stock in it. He might have good intentions and might even take steps to make sure she had enough money for the appropriate legal help, but that was it. He wasn't the type of man to take responsibility for a strange woman and her kid. He was a fuck 'em and leave 'em kind of guy.

Now, she sat with Fleur and Lucy. Lucy was Vicious's ol' lady. From what Spring understood, that was pretty much the same as being married as far as the club was concerned. She had no idea if the woman was actually married to the enforcer of the club, but it was clear from the interaction she'd seen that Vicious adored Lucy. Same as Beast worshiped Fleur.

"Mind if I join you guys?" The pretty woman approaching them had the most beautiful smile Spring had ever seen and a very round tummy.

"Not at all, Mariana," Lucy said as she got to her feet to embrace the other woman. "You feeling OK?"

Mariana smiled brightly. "I'm wonderful. When Thorn lets me lift a finger to do anything, that is. Man would have carried me out here if I hadn't set my foot down."

"Still might carry you back inside, woman." A big man in one corner of the big yard with several other men called back to her. All the women giggled. Mariana just rolled her eyes.

"Man hasn't graduated past the caveman stage," she muttered, but Spring saw the fond look she tossed his way.

"He's just worried about your pregnancy," Lucy said, squeezing her hand. "You guys weren't supposed to be trying yet."

"We weren't! But Thorn's a bit insatiable when it comes to sex, and one thing led to another and it was either wait until we got home to get a condom or say to hell with it. I didn't want to wait, and neither did he."

"I'd say you were a slut, but I'm the same way, so…" Lucy shrugged.

They all laughed.

"You guys sure aren't anything like I thought a motorcycle club would be," Spring said. "I'm not sure exactly what I expected, but this wasn't it."

Lucy shrugged. "Wait a while. When the party starts up tonight, you'll get more what you were expecting, I'd say."

That's what she was afraid of. "The party last night seemed pretty rowdy. I take it tonight's gonna be worse?"

"Probably," Fleur answered. "They've got another club coming over. Social group instead of the real deal, but it's good community relations, and it keeps them looking respectable."

"Yeah," Mariana said softly. "After what happened last year with me…"

"Not a word about that, Ana," Lucy said, reaching for Mariana and gripping her shoulder hard.

"Bastard had it coming. Only problem was that Thorn wanted to end the son of a bitch himself."

"Yeah, well, it was the best therapy I've ever had." Mariana looked haunted, but fierce.

"Do you mind if I ask what happened?" Spring hated to pry, but if she was staying here even one more night with these people, with Havoc, she needed to know.

It was Fleur who answered. "Mariana came to us after her ex-boyfriend beat her so badly she lost the child she was carrying. Bastard made a try for her again at our own clubhouse, and it didn't work out so well for him."

"I beat his head to a bloody pulp with a brick," Mariana said so softly Spring almost didn't hear her.

"And you weren't supposed to be trying to get pregnant."

"Well, Doc said it would be best to give me a little longer emotionally. My body actually healed nicely."

Mariana looked hard at Spring. "You know, if you've got a similar problem, Havoc can help you."

"We're not, like, together or anything. He's paying me to be with him this weekend." She tried to grin, thinking of a line she'd heard in a movie once. "I'm using him for sex."

Lucy spewed the soda she was drinking, prompting the rest of them to laugh uproariously. Spring grinned and tried to keep it light.

"That's awesome," Mariana said. "Totally fitting."

"Those guys all need a little something to take them down a peg or two," Lucy said as she wiped the tears of laughter from her eyes. "They all think they're irresistible to women. The club girls reinforce the idea, too."

"Club girls," Mariana sighed. "I don't mind admitting some of them intimidate me. Not saying I wouldn't fight one if I had to, but I'm sure I wouldn't come out without some damage."

"Are you kidding?" Fleur's eyes were wide. "You brained your ex. Killed him right out in the open where they all could see." She shook her head. "Sister, ain't nobody messin' with your man."

When they all laughed again, Spring couldn't help but join them. "You guys have the most twisted sense of humor."

"You stay in this place as long as we have -- which isn't really that long, yet -- you'll learn to appreciate it," Lucy said with a sigh.

"Well, after this weekend, I'm out of here."

"Right," Mariana said with a grin. "Keep telling yourself that, Spring."

"What does that mean?"

"It means," Lucy said with a grin of her own, "Havoc is all yours. He just doesn't realize it yet."

"You can't know that."

"Nope. I can't. But my man can. He says Havoc's done for. I believe him." Lucy gave Spring a little playful punch in the shoulder. "You should, too."

After that, the conversation going on around Spring faded to the background. Could Lucy be right? Did she want her to be right? No? Then why did her heart speed up and her breath catch when she thought about being Havoc's? Or, more importantly, him being hers?

* * *

Sex was a big part of the next couple of weeks. Spring had no idea how he'd managed it, but when their negotiated weekend ended, Havoc had moved her and Luca into a house a block from where the clubhouse stood.

Mostly, though, Havoc had spent time with her and Luca. When the club had called him away, he'd never stayed gone long and always, he kissed and touched her every chance he got. It was enough to make her believe what Lucy had said about Havoc being hers.

In her wildest dreams.

But it wasn't Spring's emotions that had her rattled. It was Luca's. The boy had truly fallen hard for every single member of Salvation's Bane he'd met. She couldn't say the men had been any less charmed with him. He'd ridden with every single one of them around the compound. They all made a point to play-fight and roughhouse with Luca every time they saw him. The club girls kept their distance, but two or three had made him a T-shirt with his own MC logo on the front and showered him with lipstick-covered kisses -- which he promptly wiped off, but grinned over just the same. Isadora, the club girl who was also a Domme at the BDSM club Bane owned, explained it to Spring.

"Club girls don't interfere with family. We don't try to get close, because it can be seen as an attempt to manipulate a patched member. The last thing any of them need is this bunch trying to worm their way into a family situation. Most of them are OK, but there's always one out for her own gain, and things can get really ugly. Normally, no one would have approached you, or especially Luca, but we got permission from Havoc to give him a gift." She smiled warmly. "He's a wonderful little boy."

"We appreciate your gift. I appreciate you being so nice to Luca. He loves every single person he's met."

Isadora smiled. "I'm glad. I'll do my best to keep the girls off Havoc, but you'd better lock that one down fast."

That brought Spring up short. As she watched the woman walk away, Spring had to wonder how much trouble she was really in here. The last thing she wanted to do was intrude on Havoc's life any more than she already had.

So now, two weeks later, Spring knew she had to make a decision. Luca was already too attached to everyone, but especially Havoc. He was practically glued to the man's side. When Havoc got tired of her -- and he *would* get tired of her -- where did that leave Luca?

Spring had finally found a job at the local library. It wasn't much, but it was full time. No benefits, but she could work around any future court dates she had to. Yes. It was time to go home.

She found Havoc in the backyard throwing a Nerf football with Luca. Her son was doing pretty well and obviously having so much fun it nearly made her cry. This was going to be hard. On both of them.

Spring waited until they broke for lunch before she waved Havoc over.

"Go get cleaned up, Luca," he called to the boy. "Me and your mom will be in to eat with you in a bit." Luca waved and ran off inside.

Spring saw no reason to beat around the bush. "I think it's time Luca and I get home." Not surprisingly, the words hurt.

Havoc didn't respond immediately. Instead, he sat next to her slowly, not looking at her. When he met her gaze, there was an intensity there that took Spring's breath away. "OK," he said. Spring expected at least a demand for an explanation or some kind of indication he wanted her to stay. If she'd secretly been hoping he'd try to talk her out of it, she was sorely disappointed. "When do you want to leave?"

"It would probably be best if I left tonight. I'm supposed to start at the library tomorrow. We should be settled before then."

"Do you have a place for Luca to stay while you work?"

"Fleur said she'd keep him. I'm going to drop him off at her house in the morning."

There was a long silence while Havoc studied her. Finally, he nodded curtly. "OK. We'll eat lunch, get you guys packed, and I'll follow you there to help you get settled in."

Why did this hurt so much? It was more than just leaving. It was that Havoc obviously didn't want her there. Spring knew she couldn't have it both ways. Didn't make it hurt any less.

Luca was disappointed they had to leave, but Havoc promised he could come visit any time he wanted. He also promised he'd come see him at Beast's on the days he stayed there. Spring packed in half an hour, and Havoc helped her load the few things they had into the trunk of her car.

"I can't thank you enough for everything you've done for us," Spring said softly as she and Havoc stood just inside her home. Luca had said his goodbyes and was off in his room playing. Havoc had promised the only thing that had changed was where he stayed at night. They'd still play football together almost every day. Luca had given Havoc a fierce hug before running off to his room. "You taught me a lot about myself," she continued softly. "But you really made an impression on Luca. He needed that strong male figure in his life. No matter how long it lasts, you provided that for a while, and I want you to know I appreciate it."

"I'll always be here for you if you need me, Spring. You have my phone number and the numbers of the ol' ladies and the club in your phone?" She nodded. "Use them. You need anything, I expect a call."

"I will," she said. If she stood here much longer, she was going to cry. "Well..." She cleared her throat. "Goodbye. Thanks again."

Havoc opened his mouth to say something, but closed it again. Then he nodded and turned to go. Spring watched as he started up his bike, revved it a couple of times, then took off. She watched until she could no longer see the bike or hear the roar of the pipes. Then she went to her room, curled up on her bed, and sobbed like her heart was breaking.

Because it was.

* * *

Empty. That's how Havoc felt inside as he drove away the tiny house he'd left his heart in. He wasn't leaving her alone by any means -- the two people inside that house meant more to him than anyone in the world other than his club.

Which was why he had gotten permission from Thorn to put a couple of guys on her.

Currently, Tobias and Lock were watching her and Luca. Tobias from the roof of a nearby building, Lock on the street close enough to be there if anyone threatened the two. Also, Ripper was still looking into her brother-in-law. Apparently, the man was working out a similar arrangement with another young woman, again with his wife's approval. One of many women he'd had since Spring left. The man was using his wife's desperation for a child as a way to have whatever young woman he wanted, and his wife didn't seem to mind.

He waited until he got a couple miles down the road before he stopped, pulling his bike off to the side and shutting it down. For long moments he sat there, contemplating what had just happened.

He hadn't lost her. Not completely. She was moving out to protect Luca. Havoc knew that. Not because she didn't trust his club or that she thought they'd hurt the boy emotionally, but because he'd failed to make any kind of commitment to her. Until this very moment, he wasn't even certain he could. Havoc had never wanted to tie himself down with a woman, because he believed in being faithful, and he wasn't ready for that. At least, he hadn't been. He needed to think about this. Really think about it. Because, at the moment, his first instinct was to ride as hard as he could back down that road and tell Spring she was the only woman he wanted in his life. If he did that right now, though, he couldn't be sure it was something he could follow through with. He had to make Goddamned sure he meant what he said before he said it to her. Because he wouldn't lie to her. Ever.

Decision made -- at least for the time being -- Havoc started up his bike and took off toward home. For the first time in a long time, that home was the house he'd shared with Spring and Luca. Not the clubhouse. Which unsettled him.

He pulled into the driveway and looked at the modest structure. It was comfortable for the three of them. Three bedrooms so there was an office if she needed one, two baths. Close to the clubhouse in case she needed him when he was there on club business and she was at home. Without her there, this wasn't home. It was empty. Just like his life. Like his heart.

Again, he started up his bike and rode to the Salvation's Bane compound. The clubhouse was alive with a party, as expected. Havoc parked and headed in to join the fun. Immediately, several club girls surrounded him. He grinned at first, thinking maybe this was what he needed. But as they fussed over him, Havoc knew this wasn't what he wanted.

"Thanks, girls, but I'm not interested."

"Ah, come one!" One of them, Trixie, pouted. "You've been off-limits for weeks. You can't expect us not to want to climb that delicious, muscular body of yours now that that outsider is gone. Her kid was cute, but she's not one of us. And I'm just betting she never did for you what you know we can." She giggled along with the remaining two girls.

"We can blow your mind, Havoc," Topaz insisted. "You take us up to your room, and we'll fuck and suck until you're completely satisfied. You can have us any way you want. All three of us." Again, all three giggled, as if they knew a joke and it was on him. Maybe it was. What man would turn down three beautiful women?

He would. In fact, there was no way he could see himself fucking any of them. When he imagined sex, even really hard fucking, all he saw was Spring's tight little body wrapped enticingly around his, doing every dirty, filthy thing he could conceive of. Thing was, as long as they did it in private, he knew Spring would let him do anything to her he wanted to. She trusted him that much. He wanted her that much.

"Back off." He made his voice hard and unyielding. "Not interested."

Havoc knew that wouldn't be the end of it, but he had other things to worry about. Like how he could convince Spring he wanted only her.

Chapter Eight

True to his word, Havoc had seen Luca every single day. He'd also called Spring on the days he hadn't seen her. It was almost like he… like he *cared* about her. Actually cared. Did it mean he loved her? Definitely not. Likely didn't even mean he hadn't had his share of women since Spring had been gone.

Missing Havoc was like an ache in her heart that wouldn't go away. There hadn't been a single night in the month since she'd left that she hadn't cried herself to sleep. It was disgusting the way she clung to his memory. How it felt to be in his bed. Not necessarily for sex, though she'd thought about that often enough. But just the feel of him holding her safely against his body. When he had, she'd felt like nothing in this world could harm her. When he was with her and Luca, she felt like Christopher could never take away her little boy, because Havoc was strong enough to stand between the two of them and protect them from anything. Spring wanted that back. Especially now.

She had a court date today. It was spur of the moment, which surprised her. Usually she had plenty of time to plan, so it had her nervous. It meant that either Christopher had found out about her stint in the strip club and was using it to get emergency custody, or he'd finally managed to get a judge in charge of their case he could control. Either one would be disastrous.

Because Fleur had been so wonderful about taking care of Luca for her when she worked, she hated asking her to watch the child. Still, she tried, but had been unable to get hold of either her or Havoc. Granted, she hadn't tried that hard. It wasn't an emergency. She could easily take Luca with her. It was just that knowing Luca had heard Christopher's threats had made her want to keep her son as far away from the man as she could.

Now she walked from her car toward the courthouse, ID in hand. No cell phone. Luca held her hand and was as somber as she was. The child seemed to know something was off, but hadn't questioned her the way he normally would. She'd gotten halfway up before a deep voice stopped her. A chill went down her spine, and dread filled her.

"Stop, Spring," Christopher commanded.

She hesitated, but then urged Luca to keep going. "I don't have to talk to you here, Christopher. Anything you need to say needs to be done through our lawyers in the courthouse."

"No need to get lawyers involved in this any longer. I'm taking Luca with me. Now."

Spring turned to confront him, but he was closer than she realized. He shoved her down, grabbing Luca in one strong arm. Spring went flying backward, falling and tumbling down the concrete. She screamed a split second after Luca gave a shrill cry. The little boy kicked and thrashed, trying to get down, but he was unable to break the hold of the stronger adult.

"Mommy! Mommy!"

"Luca!" She shouted as loud as she could, pushing up off the ground and sprinting for the pair. His car was just there. Feet from Christopher and Luca. She wasn't going to make it, and her phone was in her car in the opposite direction. She was sobbing now. "Luca!"

Out of nowhere, three huge bodies charged Christopher and Luca. One dove for the little boy, rolling to take the impact of the ground on his back. He let the child up and gave him a gentle shove in Spring's direction.

Havoc!

He'd come for them. How had he known they were in danger? Then she recognized Beast and Vicious. Both men confronted Christopher and kept him from following Luca. Havoc stood then. Six feet, six inches of enraged biker. Beast and Vicious let Christopher go, and he advanced on Havoc, obviously thinking he had the upper hand. Probably thought Havoc wouldn't do anything physical in public like this. Spring could have told her brother-in-law he was wrong.

There was a flash of metal before she realized Christopher had pulled a gun. She screamed just as the gun went off, the bullet hitting the brick siding on the stair rail beside Spring's head. She cried out again and rolled to the other side, scrambling to get to her feet and to Luca, who'd stopped halfway between her and the fighting men.

"Luca! Come to me!" The child glanced back at her, but only backed away from the danger instead of turning and running to her as she'd hoped.

Havoc knocked the gun away and then proceeded to beat the holy everlasting fuck out of Christopher. Blood sprayed over the sidewalk. Christopher made the mistake of fighting back, and Havoc punched the man over and over. The only sound on the crowded sidewalk was Havoc's grunts of exertion. At least, that was all Spring heard. Christopher didn't make a sound. At one point, she thought she heard someone say, "The guy shot at the woman over there. What was supposed to happen after that? If you ask me, bastard's getting what he deserved."

Havoc didn't stop once Christopher was down. He continued to pound Christopher's face, the sickening smack loud even as the crowd grew larger and larger. Spring heard several people giving accounts to each other about how Christopher had grabbed Luca and tried to run off, shoving Spring down in the process. No one attempted to pull Havoc off. Had they tried, Spring had no doubt Beast and Vicious would have diverted them in some manner.

Then Luca charged Christopher. The child ran forward, giving his own howl of rage. He sounded like a wild banshee, or some wild animal on the attack. When he was close enough, he skidded to a halt on the ground, hitting the bloody mess that had been Christopher's face several times with both fists before standing and kicking him several times. Surprisingly, it was Luca's crazed attack that seemed to pull Havoc out of his own.

Havoc scooped Luca up, murmuring to him as he hurried back to Spring. She kept her gaze on Christopher in case he pulled out another weapon. She needn't have bothered. Not only did Beast and Vicious have him restrained, but several police were in the vicinity now, thanks to the gunshot. Not that it mattered. As far as she could see, Christopher hadn't much more than moved and groaned a time or two.

Havoc reached her, setting Luca in her arms and scooping them both into his own. He was breathing hard, probably from the fight. But his body was trembling around hers. Spring would have thought the adrenaline didn't affect him like it might her after such a scuffle. But he was shaking.

"Spring, are you OK? You fell hard. Did the bullet hit you?"

"Bit scraped up, but I'm OK. I think the brick spattered my face, but nothing major. It's Luca I'm worried about."

"I'm fine, Mom," he said, his skinny arms around her neck. "Havoc was right there, just like he said he would be."

"I know, baby. We owe him *everything*."

"I'm going to collect, too," he said ominously. "You owe me everything, and I'm taking it." His arms tightened around her, and he buried his face in her hair. "Let's get the fuck outta here."

* * *

He'd almost lost her. Almost lost Luca. *Not again!* When that bastard Christopher had fired the fucking gun, Havoc had nearly lost his mind. He'd risked a glance over his shoulder when he heard Spring scream and had seen her rolling out of the way. He'd only hoped she hadn't been hit. Luca had crouched between his mother and danger instead of running for Spring like he'd hoped he would, but, strangely, it had made him fiercely proud of the child even as it terrified him beyond imagining. It was like history was repeating itself. The child didn't look like he'd frozen in fear either. He'd looked like he was going to defend his mother at all costs.

Havoc made it to a bench close to the steps before collapsing into it, Spring and Luca piled up in his lap. He held both of them tightly. What surprised him the most was the state his body was in. He couldn't seem to stop trembling. It was embarrassing, really. He was a battle-hardened vice president of a dangerous bunch of men. Yet, this tiny woman and her son held such a tight hold on his heart that he nearly panicked when they were in danger. And it wasn't anything he didn't have under control. The second Christopher had approached them on the stairs, he'd put his men into motion.

"Thank God we were following you," he murmured to her as he helped her and Luca into his big F-350. The police would definitely be hunting for them soon, and Havoc hoped to make a getaway before that. He'd probably get into more trouble than he was already in, but he didn't want to stress Spring or Luca any more than they already were.

"Sir? Sir!"

"Fuck," Havoc muttered. "Fuckin' figures."

"It's not like you didn't know you'd have to talk to them," Spring said with a small smile. "Let's just get this over with now."

Havoc turned, sure death was still in his eyes, especially when the first officer backed up a step. His partner was close behind him and gave no sign he was intimidated. He wasn't disrespectful either, as some cops could be with bikers. Havoc's respect for the man was immediate.

"We need to talk to you before you leave, sir," the second cop said. "I'm sorry. I know you just want to get your family away from all this, but you did beat a man nearly to death."

"I'd say it woulda been different if he hadn't pulled that gun, but the second he grabbed Luca, he was gettin' a beatin'."

The cop actually grinned. "Can't say I blame you. Do you mind if I ask your relationship to the young woman and the child?"

"She's my fiancée. Kid's hers, but I'll be adoptin' him the second we're married."

"I understand. What happened?"

Havoc nodded at Spring, whose lips were parted in kissable surprise. Something he'd remedy when he got her home. "Guy's Luca's father. It's a complicated matter, but the bottom line is she had a court date today. Spur of the moment. I got my brothers lookin', and the bastard lured her here. There was no court date. He got his lawyer to contact her directly. Haven't talked to Spring to actually find out what happened, but my guess is, she was so panicked at the quick summons she didn't take time to confirm with her lawyer."

"That's accurate," Spring said in a soft voice. He glanced at her, and she sent him an apologetic smile. Her cheeks were bright red. He wasn't sure if it was embarrassment or something to do with him claiming her the way he had, but it was a becoming look either way.

"You ain't got nothin' to be sorry for, woman," Havoc snapped. "This was his fault. Not yours. Wish you'd called me, though. We'll address that when we get home. Don't worry. Won't be a mistake you make again."

"I tried --"

"Not hard enough!"

"You're sounding all mean and growly, Havoc," Luca said in reprimand. "Don't be mean to my mommy."

Havoc took a deep breath and grinned at the child. "Yeah, well, you and me got stuff to talk about, too." He winked at the kid, and Luca grinned at him, not in the least intimidated. "I didn't see the events leadin' up to him grabbing Luca, but we saw Spring's car and were looking for her. Got there just as he shoved Spring down the stairs. I'm sure you heard the rest already."

"Well, I got three accounts that match almost exactly. All of them put you as the defender. I can't say there won't be more questions, but that should do for now." The officer pointed to Havoc's hands. "You might want to get those looked at. You, too, ma'am. Looks like you got hit by the brick shrapnel."

"Got help at home. Can we go now?" Havoc knew he sounded impatient, but he really wanted to get Spring and Luca home.

Then something hit him. The cop had called them "your family." Spring. And Luca. *Family*. Yeah, they were as much of his life as his brothers. The thought still ringing in his head, he hopped in the big truck and started it. Once his seat belt was on, he just sat there, waiting for the panic he'd always associated with a woman laying some kind of claim on him. After his ex-wife, he'd wanted nothing to do with any kind of a relationship. Now, he couldn't imagine *not* having Spring in his life. As his wife. His ol' lady.

He turned his head to look at Spring's anxious face.

"Are you angry with me?" Her lower lip quivered, and it looked like his feelings mattered to her. Not at all like Lori had during their marriage.

"No, baby. I have concerns, but it's nothing to be worried about. Ain't sayin' I ain't gonna whip your ass, but that's a discussion for later." He grinned at her.

"Is that 'cause that man got me? 'Cause I'm sure Mommy didn't mean to let him get me."

"Honey, you know I'm not gonna hurt your mom. And no. She didn't do it on purpose. That's something for me and her to discuss." He faced Luca directly then, making sure the boy held his gaze. "You and I will discuss what you did, though. Your job was to protect your mom. Mine was to take care of the bad guy. I didn't need you to help me take him out."

"I know, but I just felt like it." Luca didn't back down an inch, looking Havoc straight in the eyes. He couldn't have been prouder if Luca had been his own kid. "No one hurts my mommy."

Havoc gave a sharp nod. What else could he say? He felt the same way, so how could he fault the child? "I understand. From now on, though, you let me do the heavy lifting. Me and my brothers are always the front line. If we fail, then it's up to you. You stick close to your mom and protect her from anything we can't."

The child seemed to consider that for a long moment, then finally he nodded slowly. "I can do that."

"Good." Because no way anything else would get past him or his brothers. They would always be a solid wall between them and the people they loved. "Let's go home. Luca, you mind stayin' with Beast and Fleur for a couple of hours? Me and your mom need some time to talk."

"You mean about what you said? About adopting me?"

"Yep. I gotta convince her it's the right thing to do."

"Please, Mom?"

Spring sighed. "We have a lot to talk about first, honey. I'm not promising anything."

Luca looked back at him, and Havoc grinned. "Don't worry, big guy. I'll convince her."

Luca gave him a stern look. "You better. I need strong role models in my life."

Havoc couldn't help but chuckle at that. Apparently, the kid listened to everything. Havoc found that, where it had never mattered to him before, he wanted to be the one to teach this kid. He wanted to be that role model.

They dropped Luca off at the Beast's home. The enforcer pulled in right behind Havoc and took Luca.

"You good with stayin' with me and Fleur tonight, buddy?"

"Only if you let Fleur cook the pancakes tomorrow morning."

Beast growled and started tickling the little boy before throwing him over his shoulder and heading to the house.

Havoc reached for Spring's hand and squeezed. "You good, baby?"

"I don't know," she said. "How much of what you said back there did you actually mean?"

He reached for her and grasped her face in his big hands. "Every fuckin' word, baby. You're gonna be my wife, my ol' lady. And I'm makin' Luca my son."

"You know I'll never consent to any of that if we're not exclusive. I can't stand the thought of sharing you with another woman. I know some men in this lifestyle would have a wife and not think anything of having sex with any number of women hanging around their clubhouse. I saw that at the party you had me watch."

"You did. But none of those men had women of their own. Vicious was there, as was Thorn, but both of them had their women with them. They'd never be unfaithful, and neither would I."

"At the same time, I don't want you to be miserable. You've lived a long time in this kind of life. Can you really change your mindset so suddenly this late in the game?"

"You spilled your story to me at the beach. When we get home, I'm gonna tell you mine. It shaped my past and who I am, but, honey, believe me when I tell you, no matter anything in my past, you've shaped my future."

Chapter Nine

Spring tried not to get too excited. She didn't want to let her heart believe this was real, but finally acknowledged it was too late. Being with Havoc was what she wanted. If that meant she had to take a chance and believe what he said, then she was going to do it. It was what was right for her and what was right for Luca. Havoc had proven he'd take care of her little boy and would never abandon him, no matter what Spring did. He'd do it and be civil about it.

The time apart from him had probably been the best thing she could have done for herself in that she saw how he acted when they'd separated. He hadn't pushed her, but he'd done exactly as he'd promised. He'd kept contact with them, he'd seen Luca every single day he could, and he'd even watched over them without her realizing it. He might be wild at heart, but Havoc was a good man.

When they reached the house, Havoc hurried around to her side of the truck and snagged her hand when she shut the door. He led her inside then pulled her to him and wrapped his big, strong arms tightly around her.

"I've missed you, woman," he said gruffly.

"I've missed you, too." Tears threatened, and Spring tried valiantly to hold them back. It didn't go any good. Soon, she was sobbing against his wide chest. Havoc just rubbed her back and buried his face in her hair.

"I'm here, baby. Whatever I did to run you off, I'm sorry. I should have told you I wanted you with me."

"Later," she said. "We can talk about it later." Spring slid her arms around his neck and tilted her face up for his kiss.

The second they settled together, everything inside Spring relaxed. She loved the way he kissed her. There was a mixture of tenderness and need she found endearing. Like he was hungry for her but unwilling to scare her off with that same need. She whimpered, opening her mouth for his sweeping tongue, which she met with her own.

"Need you, baby," he said between thrusts of his tongue. "You gonna let me have you?"

"Anything you want, Havoc."

"Good. Need some things from you you ain't gonna like, but you're gonna do them anyway." He growled at her before lifting her, urging her legs around his waist. Carrying her to the bedroom, he swatted her ass a couple of times through her skirt. "That's just the beginning, woman. You're in a heap of trouble."

"Havoc! What are you doing?" She wanted to be outraged. Instead, there was more than a little interest as her ass stung where he'd swatted her.

"You think I was kidding when I told Luca I was gonna spank you?"

"Well, yeah. What'd I do?"

"You didn't call me when you got the court summons."

"But I did! I called both you and Fleur to try to get someone to keep Luca while I was gone! Neither of you answered, and I didn't have time to wait!"

"How long have you been in court battles with that fucker? Since Luca was born?" He sat on the bed, keeping her in his lap facing him. Spring could feel his erection pressing instantly through his jeans and her panties.

"Pretty much. Yes."

"In all that time, how many times have you been called to court immediately? No warning whatsoever?"

"Well, none."

"Exactly."

"But I thought maybe he'd filed some kind of emergency thing because he'd found out about me dancing at the club, or the arrangement you and I'd had before. I thought it might be a social services thing where he was filing for emergency custody." The more she tried to rationalize it, the more she realized how she should have seen through the ruse. A desperate attempt for Christopher to get her out somewhere she wouldn't cause a fuss so he could take Luca without a fight. And he'd nearly won.

"I can tell by the look on your face you know better. Why didn't you call your lawyer?"

"I-I don't know. I just assumed she'd be there when I got inside, waiting to tell me what was going on."

"Is that something she'd normally have done?"

Spring winced. "No. She'd have locked down the reason for the urgent summons in the first place."

"Right." He frowned at her. "So, back to my original question. Why didn't you call me?"

"I already told you --"

"You said you tried. How many times, Spring?"

"Well, once. I guess." She looked down, picking at his T-shirt in her nervousness.

"You guess?"

"Fine, Havoc. Once. I called once. When you didn't answer, I didn't leave a voicemail or text you because I didn't want to bother you, and you don't answer text messages."

"I would have for you. And with Fleur?"

"Same." Spring met his gaze with her angry one. "I might be her friend, but I don't expect anyone to drop what they're doing to come to my rescue. Luca is my responsibility. I wasn't going to force him on her."

Havoc sighed, looking disappointed. That hurt worse than the thought of him being angry with her. "Did it ever occur to you that you've made more than a few friends at Salvation's Bane? Fleur was your friend before. How would she feel if she heard you say that?"

Well, when he put it that way. Fleur was a wonderful person and an even better friend. "I wouldn't want to tell her I said that," Spring said softly, suddenly ashamed she'd doubted her friend.

"I can understand your reservations about bothering me. I gave you no reason to think I was approachable like that. But you should have trusted Fleur to have your back. You know she loves you."

"Yes," she said. "I guess I was just panicked and maybe being a little stubborn. I wanted to prove to myself I didn't need *you*."

"In doing so, you put Luca at risk. Not to mention yourself."

"I get you. I'm sorry. It won't happen again."

"Nope," he said, maneuvering her around so she lay over his lap. Dread settled deep in the pit of her stomach, and Spring struggled.

"What are you doing? Let me up!"

"What does it feel like I'm doing, little flower?"

"Havoc!"

Somehow, he got her panties down and her skirt up. The next thing she knew, Havoc brought his hand down on her ass. Hard.

"Oww! What was that for?"

"For putting yourself and your son at unnecessary risk." He did it again, this time on the other side. And again. *Smack! Smack! Smack!*

"Stop! *Havoc*!" She squirmed, struggling as hard as she could to get away from the stinging smack of his hand. Havoc held her firmly, having to get her legs between his so he could hold her steady as he continued to rain his hand on her bare ass over and over.

"Don't think for one minute," he said in between swats of his hand, "that I'm ever going to let you get away with bullshit like you did today. You took ten years off my life! You knew better, but you panicked."

"I promise!" she wailed. "I swear! I'll never do it again!"

"You panic for any reason, you call me. You leave messages, you text, you call the clubhouse or any of the ol' ladies. I believe asked you if you had them before I left here. Right?"

"Yes," she gasped as he brought his hand down yet again. "You did."

"Did you lie? Did you not have them?"

"No! I just didn't use them! I didn't want to bother anyone!"

"Never again, Spring. You have all kinds of ways to get in touch with me. You use every single one of them." He finally stopped, pulling her back into position across his lap, her legs straddling him. His palms cupped her burning ass gently. "In this situation, you don't leave the house until you've made contact with me or my brothers. We'll take care of it. If nothing else, one of us would have taken you to the courthouse so you weren't by yourself. Honey…" He slid his hands up to her face. "You're not alone. You're part of us now. Salvation's Bane takes care of its own.

Members and ol' ladies and children. You're one of us. Part of our family."

"I didn't think most clubs worked like that."

Havoc gave her an impatient look. "Most clubs probably don't. But we do. You get me?"

"I get you, Havoc." She pursed her lips. "But did you really have to spank me?"

He chuckled, warm and deep, pulling her tightly against him. "I did, little flower. And it will be repeated as necessary. You don't like it? My suggestion would be not to repeat the same mistake."

Spring peeked up at him and squirmed a little. Her ass hurt, but there was something else as well. Havoc studied her a minute before he slid one hand back down to her ass, then between her cheeks and to the opening of her pussy. Then he gave her a big, wicked grin.

"Could it be that you... *liked* your punishment?"

* * *

The first thought in Spring's mind was a resounding "no!" It had hurt, Goddammit! She wouldn't be lying at all. Would she? That brief hesitation on her part was her answer. Yeah. There was a tiny part of her that had gotten off on his dominance.

"Maybe I did. Doesn't mean I'm eager to repeat it." And Spring had the suspicion there was more to his need to spank her than he was letting on. "Now, as much as I want to get on with this reunion --"

"Oh, so you think you're gonna get to come after your punishment?"

"Absolutely," she said firmly. "Because this isn't something we've ever talked about, and you just took a huge liberty." She tried to look stern but wasn't sure she pulled it off. Especially when she shivered just thinking about it. And when her ass still throbbed under the palms cupping her cheeks.

He chuckled. "Fair enough. Doesn't mean it will always happen. Now. What're you getting at?"

"What other reason did you spank me for? Because I have a feeling that was more than a little personal, and not all about me or Luca."

To her surprise, Havoc stilled, then gave a defeated sigh. He slid his arms back around her and settled them both on the bed so she was draped over him. For long moments they lay there. Spring was beginning to think he wasn't going to tell her, and she wasn't asking again. Then he started to speak.

"Not really much to tell. The night we met was the anniversary of my son's death."

She gasped. It had been the last thing she'd expected. Pushing up so she could look at him, she said, "I'm so sorry, Havoc. I never meant to pry."

"Don't be sorry." He urged her head back to his chest. "Shoulda told you a while ago. My boy would have been sixteen. He was eight when he passed. Died while I was in Afghanistan. Not sure exactly when he started gettin' sick, but it was a few months before my wife took him for treatment. He had leukemia. Needed a bone marrow transplant. From what I was able to piece together, she never tried to get ahold of my commanding officer -- and I always made sure she had the correct numbers -- nor did she go through the Red Cross to get me an emergency leave. She didn't try to get in touch with me at all until he was gone."

He took a breath and trembled around her. "I did some digging, figuring it was my right as his father to see what happened from the time he was admitted until he died several months later. Looking back, I think I just wanted to punish myself for not being there. Anyway, in looking for a bone marrow match, they did go through the VA to get the records of my blood type. Now, I don't understand all the medical stuff, but apparently my blood type and Grayson's blood type weren't compatible for a match. In fact, from what I could tell, our blood types indicated there was no way I was Gray's biological father."

Spring couldn't help the little catch in her breathing. "That must have been very hard."

"Not as hard as knowing I hadn't been there when he needed me. His mother obviously had cared more about hiding her secret than she did about our son, and that hurt, too. I'd raised Gray as my own and, in my mind, he still was mine. If I'd known, I'd have gotten together every single buddy I'd made in the service and every single one of them would have tested to see if they were a potential match as a donor. At that point, I could have cared less if she'd had an affair. I just wanted my son back."

"I can see why it's important for me to always let you know if there's a problem. Why you made sure I had every phone number available to someone who could find you."

"I'm sorry, Spring. I should have told you earlier, but it isn't something I talk about with anyone. Only Stryker knows about Grayson, and even he doesn't know all the details." He took a breath and continued.

"Is there more?"

He shrugged. "Only that Olivia served me with divorce papers exactly one year later. Bitch always had to be the center of my attention. I've always thought that that was one of the reasons she didn't call me. Deep down, I think she wanted to spring the fact that I wasn't Gray's father at a time of her choosing. One where it would gain her the most advantage. Him getting sick meant that, if I got there to be with Gray, her revelation wouldn't matter to me because I loved Gray so much. I'd love to say I was wrong, but that's just the type of person Olivia is."

"That's cold, Havoc. How could a mother do that to her child?"

"Beats the living fuck outta me, baby."

They lay there for a long time. Spring rubbed her palm back and forth over his shoulder, loving the feel of his muscles under his shirt. She was acutely aware her bare bottom was still very much on display. Havoc's big hand rubbed gently over the abused flesh. She shivered a little at the memory of how it had gotten so sore.

"Hm," he rumbled beneath her. "I think you're still feeling the effects of your spanking."

"Well, yeah. My ass is sore, you ape!"

He chuckled. "Ain't what I meant, flower." He reached down again, his finger tracing the seam of her ass all the way to her pussy. He brought his wet finger to his mouth. "Mmmm… Delicious."

"Havoc!"

"What? I like your cream. Want more."

"Not sure I can lay on my back. You ensured I won't be sitting comfortably for a good long while."

"You have no idea how that thought satisfies me."

"You really are an ape." She play-slapped at his shoulder, but he just chuckled.

Havoc reached to the nightstand and pulled out a condom. He tore it open, then reached around her to sheath himself.

"I didn't think you'd want to use a condom," Spring said, a little confused.

"Don't. But you can't use birth control, and we've not talked about this. Ain't come in you since that time in the ocean, and I won't until you're ready. 'Cause once I do, I'll be fuckin' you every fuckin' night until you're pregnant with my kid. So be ready to be pregnant again before you tell me you want my cum."

His talk sent a thrill through her. He was right. They definitely needed to have that conversation, and now wasn't the time. Spring had a feeling it wouldn't be long though.

Before she could think more about it, he slid inside her in one sure stroke. His satisfied growl mingled with her own sigh. There was a little resistance, but she was so wet he slid right inside her with no pain.

"Still can't get over how fuckin' tight you are, baby."

"Feels so good, Havoc."

"Damn straight it does. Gonna feel even better soon. You don't come until I tell you to."

"What? Havoc!"

"You heard me. Don't you dare come until I say. You do, there'll be more spankings."

"Oh, God!" Spring felt her pussy contracting, squeezing Havoc as he surged inside her. "Why would you do that? I can't control when I come!"

"You can and you will. Unless you want another spanking."

She groaned. "My poor ass couldn't take it."

"Then I guess you'll just have to suck it up. Hold on until I tell you. I promise it will be worth it."

Spring just nodded, unable to say anything. Havoc gripped her hips and moved her to the pace he wanted, surging up as he pulled her down on him. He hit deep inside her. The pleasure built with every stroke.

He shifted them so they were on their sides, protecting her from rolling on her abused ass. Spring was thankful, too, because that would have doused any fire he'd been stoking on the spot. She hadn't been kidding when she told him it hurt. Though, she had the feeling he'd meant it to. Once on their sides, Havoc urged her leg over his hips and took complete control. Over and over he thrust, pounding deep with each stroke. Harder. Faster.

Shifting a little, Havoc cupped her breast and fastened his mouth over one puckered nipple. Spring cried out, the sensation nearly pushing her over the edge.

"Havoc! Please!"

"Not yet. You hold on a little longer."

"I -- Havoc, I can't!"

He growled against her chest, his other big palm splayed wide over her back to hold her against him. Just when Spring thought she couldn't hold back any longer, Havoc slid his hand down her body to gently cup her ass and moved her to put just the perfect amount of pressure on her clit.

"Now, baby. Come for me."

She did. A wet wave of pleasure gushed through her, clamping down on Havoc's cock and making her pussy throb that much more.

"God, baby," he grunted. "I feel you squeezing me!"

"Oh, my God! Havoc!"

Soon, he joined her, yelling his completion to the ceiling. He pulsed inside her several times before his cock stilled. Then he rolled to his back, instead of covering her with his own body as she knew he loved to do.

"Should have told you before, Spring," he said. "I love you. I'll always be faithful to you."

"Oh…" She hadn't expected that, and she knew he knew it. Probably why he waited until she wasn't prepared for it. He seemed to like to keep her off balance sometimes.

"What?" he demanded. "Bikers can love, too, you know."

"Never doubted it," she managed to get out, but her voice caught. "I just… I didn't expect you to…"

"Admit it?"

"Well, yeah."

"I wouldn't. Not with anyone but you or Luca."

"Do you really mean to adopt Luca? Christopher will probably make a fuss, since he's the biological father."

"Don't worry about Christopher. I have the feeling he'll let this one go."

"Do I want to know?"

"Probably not."

Spring giggled, happier than she could remember being in a very long while. "Fuck him then," she declared. "If it's what you want, I know Luca would want it, too."

"Yeah." He chuckled. "Fuck Christopher. And yeah. It's what I want. But. I'm fifteen years older than you. You OK with that?"

"Yes, Havoc. I'm good with our age difference. But don't think I won't use every opportunity I have to tease you about your age. I'm looking forward to it, actually."

"Braxton."

She stilled. "What?"

"My name," he said. "Braxton Anderson. Brax for short."

She looked up at him. "I suppose I should have asked you about that a long time ago."

"No. Was my job to tell you. And you're right. Should have told you that our first weekend together."

"Well, I know now. Besides, Havoc suits you better."

"You think so?"

"Yep. But honestly. I don't care what I call you as long as I can call you mine."

He grinned up at her, leaning up to kiss her softly. "You can always call me yours, flower. Always."

Marteeka Karland

Marteeka Karland is an international bestselling author who leads a double life as an erotic romance author by evening and a semi-domesticated housewife by day. Known for her down and dirty MC romances, Marteeka takes pleasure in spinning tales of tenacious, protective heroes and spirited, vulnerable heroines. She staunchly advocates that every character deserves a blissful ending, even, sometimes, the villains in her narratives. Her writings are speckled with intense, raw elements resulting in page-turning delight entwined with seductive escapades leading up to gratifying conclusions that elicit a sigh from her readers.

Away from the keyboard, Marteeka finds joy in baking and supporting her husband with their gardening activities. The late summer season is set aside for preserving the delightful harvest that springs from their combined efforts (which is mostly his efforts, but you can count it). To stay updated with Marteeka's latest adventures and forthcoming books, make sure to visit her website. Don't forget to register for her newsletter which will pepper you with a potpourri of Teeka's beloved recipes, book suggestions, autograph events, and a plethora of interesting tidbits.

Marteeka at Changeling: changelingpress.com/marteeka-karland-a-39

Changeling Press E-Books

More Sci-Fi, Fantasy, Paranormal, and BDSM adventures available in e-book format for immediate download at ChangelingPress.com -- Werewolves, Vampires, Dragons, Shapeshifters and more -- Erotic Tales from the edge of your imagination.

What are E-Books?

E-books, or electronic books, are books designed to be read in digital format -- on your desktop or laptop computer, notebook, tablet, Smart Phone, or any electronic e-book reader.

Where can I get Changeling Press E-Books?

Changeling Press e-books are available at ChangelingPress.com, Amazon, Apple Books, Barnes & Noble, and Kobo/Walmart.

ChangelingPress.com

Printed in Great Britain
by Amazon